Ackn

First and foremost, I would like to express my deepest gratitude in collaborating with my Cousin, Alan Cohen.

This Book is dedicated in memory to my beautiful, Sister, Edie Black. When Edie was killed, November 2015, I was heartbroken. Edie had this book started and it was my goal to complete this in her memory. There were days I found this challenging to work on her book. Many people rose to the occasion to give me the boost I needed to rework and edit this story. A heartfelt thank you to my Husband, my rock, Joe Nunes who showed me love, support and helped me succeed in finishing this book. Thank you to Rosemary Pellegrini and Phyllis Hargreaves who generously gave me the suggestions and offered support in helping me finish the book. After the trial, I was able to pick up the pieces.

I would like to thank my Co-Writer, Alan Cohen for his support. With your ideas, you have steered this book to completion.

For those of you who touched Edie's life in any way, you know who you are. Alan and I look forward to your comments from all the readers.

****

Edie, I enjoyed seeing how you blossomed from child to young lady. I enjoyed seeing you transform from college to a professional, to a mother. You were an extraordinary lady whose smile always brightened everyone's day. I enjoyed working on your manuscript. It gave me the opportunity to see another side of you – the imaginative writer that you have become.

I miss you and think of you often. You are never far from my thoughts. Some people live a long life and never touch the lives they encounter. Although your life was tragically cut short, you always made a positive difference in the lives of everyone you met.

Chapter 1: The Beginning – June 2005

If we were to go one step further, the definition for obsession which I feared my puppy love was bordering is described as the state of being obsessed with someone or something, or an idea or thought that continually preoccupies or intrudes on a person's mind.

I was 6 when I first met Heather Cort and her Kennedyesque, larger-than-life family. To say I was smitten would be putting it lightly. Despite our differences and my seemingly inferior status, we became best friends and the Corts became like my second family. Yet nothing, and I mean nothing, could have prepared me for her two brothers, Matt and Brian Cort. And so, my story begins…

***

Scientists say that if you lie on a hot sidewalk, the energy moves directly to your body. I was no scientist, but it was so hot you probably could have fried an egg on the sidewalk. The six-month stretch from January to June was the warmest ever. Temperatures were sizzling which was especially evident on this oppressive June evening. When I closed my eyes, I could feel the sweltering heat on my skin.

"Are you daydreaming again?" My mom said, snapping her fingers.

"I'm sorry?" I asked. "Did I miss something?"

My mother gestured to my bedroom window. "Heather is honking her horn for you. You'd better hurry. Have fun tonight!" She said and closed the door.

I quickly rubbed the last drop of my tingly cold mint perfume oil on my wrists. It felt nice, like rubbing ice cubes. The heat wave was intense, and my room felt unbearably hot. I fumbled with my overnight bag and thanked my lucky stars that Heather's house had central air conditioning. We were celebrating our last day of classes as well as our freedom, at least for the summer, from high school. We were now officially seniors! The countdown had begun…one year until graduation.

Heather Cort and I met in first grade during recess when mean-spirited Alex Lucas asked me if I was a boy. "Is your name Sam? That's a boy's name!" he howled. My eyes filled with tears, but then I heard the lovely blonde little girl defend me. "For your information her name is Samantha, which is a beautiful name. Why don't you scram before I tell the teacher that you KICKED ME ALEX LUCAS! By the way, your name is also a girl's name, he snickered.

We watched Alex Lucas retreat and I shuffled my feet uncertainly.

She smiled. "I'm Heather Cort."

I nodded, shyly.

"Come on." She took my hand and led me to the hopscotch court. "Let's play!"

From that day forward, we were always together. I admired Heather immediately, quickly giving her the pet name "BBB." What did "BBB" stand for you might ask? The three B's stood for blonde, beautiful and bold. Although in later years, I often replaced bold with bossy. But even with her bossy tendencies Heather was my idol.

The word *no* was not in Heather's vocabulary and she didn't give a rat's ass about following the rules. Over the years, she had become something of a wild child, often sneaking out of the house after curfew and dating a variety of boys from poetic, sensitive types to bad boy rockers. I on the other hand was the good girl tag along. We were still thick as thieves, but I knew that she would probably get me into trouble one day. But a little mischief was good for a seventeen-year-old teenager; at least, that's what I kept telling myself.

I heard the honking of the horn again and slung my bag over my shoulder. *God, Heather was impatient!* As I approached her car, I heard her shout from the driver's window. "Holy ****, Batman! Are you wearing heels? *Dang* Sam, you look HOT tonight!"

Will you be quiet before someone hears you, I hissed? it's only shorts and a tank top.

Yeah, tiny white transparent shorts and a barely-there tank-top. I'm glad to see that you finally have TITS - she exclaimed loudly.

What - I panicked. Maybe, I should change. Calm down little Sammy. Are you ready for a good time tonight? So, what are we doing? We are going to the Boat Shack, Heather declared.

We're never get in as I don't have a fake ID. Yes, we will Sam. Don't worry. Skippy is at the door and he's friends with Matt, Heather said in her bossy, know-it-all voice.

I didn't feel like arguing with Heather and even if I did, I knew I wouldn't win. As we drove there, Heather prattled on about boys, school, and summer vacation while I listened and looked for cool tunes on the radio.

So, is Matt home from Stanford yet? I asked, trying to sound indifferent.

"You are so crushing on him. Brian is going to be heartbroken if he finds out. Especially after that kiss."

I blushed at the memory of the kiss, but quickly protested, I am not crushing on Matt. If anyone is crushing on anyone's brother, we both know that you have it bad for Pete.

Well, Pete is easy on the eyes, Heather agreed. But my dance card is pretty full these days and I'm seeing Ryan. About that - Where is Ryan tonight, I asked. Don't get angry Sam, but he might come by the Boat Shack later with some of his buddies. What - You promised me a boy-free night!

Heather grinned and gave me a sly wink. *"Puh-lease."* Sam. Promises like that are meant to be broken.

"Whatever," I said rolling my eyes at her.

Heather was confident and self-assured and very tenacious.. She used her considerable beauty, brains and charm to get whatever she wanted. Come to think of it, the apple didn't fall to far from the tree. If I were a gambler, when it came to the Cort family, I'd know never to bet against them.

Heather recognized from an early age that she was drop-dead gorgeous. She had always been a pretty girl, but after she got her period at the age of fourteen, she suddenly sprouted giant breasts and then next came her curves. She was a blue-eyed blonde vivacious "hottie" with a sweetheart ass. Heather was every boy's wet dream and every girl's worst nightmare.

I, on the other hand, was a late bloomer. I had always considered myself an athletic tomboy with no chest. It was only until very recently, that it had all changed. I first became aware of my sex appeal last September when I was late for gym class. I was alone in the locker room changing, and quickly threw on my shorts and tank top. As I was running up the deserted stairwell to the gym, I ran into Chris Porter, quarterback and total hunk.

"Nice legs," he drawled in what could only be described in a seductive voice.

I was speechless and for the millionth time, I wished that I could come up with a pithy reply like the Corts always did. Instead, I just blushed and mumbled "thanks" under my breath. I was such an IDIOT.

Anyway, I went from boyfriend less with virtually no male attention to suddenly being a hot commodity. At first, I just shrugged it off, especially compliments from parents, relatives, and other grown-ups, like "You look like a model, dear." I would smile politely, but it went in one ear, and out the other. Quite frankly, I thought they were all crazy. It wasn't until I overheard my brother Peter, who was one year older with his buddies talking about me that my opinion about myself slowly started to change. "Come on man, your sister is hot. Why can't I ask her out?" I knew the voice, it was Steve Jones, and he was cute, I mean really cute. "No way Steve, stay away from my sister."

Soon after, I noticed that Brian Cort was acting different around me and when he invited me to his senior prom, I almost fainted. Brian was one year older, and like all members of the Cort (i.e. SEX GOD) family, he was absurdly good-looking, but Brian was like a brother to me, so I pushed all romantic fantasies aside. It wasn't that I was oblivious to Brian's charm and good looks; I was a teenage girl with raging hormones after all. But he was off limits, because he was Heather's brother, my *bro pal,* and good friends with my brother, Peter. If that wasn't deal breaker enough, then I didn't know what was.

In the end, I did go with Brian to his senior prom, and we even shared a kiss. Yes, that's right, we kissed! I didn't intend to. It's just that, uh, he surprised me. And…umm…he had PUCKER POWER! Despite that, I have stayed away from him.

You might be scratching your head asking why would I stay away from my *bro pal* who was a sex god with pucker power? The reason was simple - his name *was* Matthew Cort.

Chapter 2: Eight Years later – May 2013

"Professor Sapra!" I yelled LOUDLY as my voice echoed through the massive lobby capturing the attention of everyone, including the conference attendees streaming out of the auditorium. My cheeks reddened from the unwanted attention, but I chose to ignore it, as I saw Vijay's head pop up from the crowd.

"Samantha" he yelled out while ushering me over with a wave.

I made my way through the sea of people, stopping when I finally reached him -Professor Sapra, you dropped your passport. What - he mumbled. I'm beyond embarrassed. Thank you, Samantha. You are a godsend. I breathed a sigh of relief. No problem, I'm glad that I caught up to you in time. Nodding his head and smiling, that's an understatement, he agreed. Now that you're here, let me introduce you.

The Professor continued, turning me toward what appeared to be a small army of "Masters of the Universe" type men who were all clad in very expensive looking suits, reeking of big money and overconfidence. Gentlemen, this is Samantha Nottingham. She is one of the best and brightest interns that I've ever had. I'm sad to report that this is her last week with me in London as she is returning to America next week. In fact, Samantha contributed greatly to the presentation that we were just discussing on Virtual Currency and the Future of Bitcoins.

A few murmured hellos and compliments on my work with the presentation. I nodded to one or two, and was just about to strike up a conversation with a gray-haired gentleman when I turned to the sound of my voice being called - "Samantha" I suddenly looked at the men in the group to find the source of the distinct male voice and a familiar pair of blue eyes caught mine - Mr. Cort

"You two know each other," Vijay asked, looking between us.

I was stunned by his appearance but desperately tried to appear unfazed. I dropped my gaze from Mr. Cort and shifted uncomfortably, turning my attention to Professor Sapra. "Yes, Mr. Cort is a close family friend. In fact, his children were my best friends growing up." Where did you grow up again, Vijay asked? Um, in Marblehead, Massachusetts.

Professor Sapra's brow was furrowed like he was confused. "MARBLE? HEAD?" He smirked. "Is that a real town?" It most certainly is Vijay. Thomas Cort answered for the both of us – it's 16 miles northeast of Boston. Hmm…was that the birthplace of the American Navy, Vijay inquired. Mr. Cort nodded; I'm impressed Vijay…you certainly know your history. Although, what Marblehead is really known for is sailing.

I grinned sheepishly. "That's true." Then I hesitantly added, "It was actually Mr. Cort's son, Matt, who taught me to sail when I was only eight years old."

For the briefest moment, Mr. Cort's expression clouded over, and he seemed like he was concerned about something, but it was quickly replaced by a hearty smile as he turned to the other gentleman in the group. "I'm sorry gentlemen, we've been totally remiss leaving you out of the conversation."

"Not at all Tom. Catch up with your friend and we will see you later for cocktails," replied one of the men from the group as they all shook hands leaving Mr. Cort, Vijay, and me alone.

"I should go as well as I need to catch a plane and I feel like I'm intruding on your reunion," Vijay said while shaking Thomas Cort's hand good-bye. Then he turned to me and gave me an unexpected hug. "I will miss you Samantha. I wish I could persuade you to stay in London, but I know that we've been over this already. Take care of yourself and if you need any help with the job hunt, please let me know."

"I will Professor Sapra, thank you," I responded returning his hug.

"And then there were two." Mr. Cort joked as we watched Professor Sapra walk away.

"I have so many questions for you Mr. Cort, that I don't know where to begin!" I exclaimed happily.

"Me too, Sam. This is such a huge surprise and you are so grown up and so beautiful; wait until Catherine and the kids see you! Can you join us for dinner?"

My voice faltered for a moment. "Umm … is the whole family here in London with you?"

"Yes, and they will be thrilled to see you again. How long has it been?"

A shiver ran down my spine and my heart started to race at the prospect of seeing the entire Cort family again. *Get a grip Sam!*

"E…et years," I mumbled, awkwardly, clearing my throat.

"What was that, Sam?"

"It's been eight years, sir."

I felt him looking at me. "That's a long time Sam."

Straightening my shoulders, I finally locked eyes with Mr. Cort, and just nodded. I had so many questions that I wanted to ask, but I didn't want to overwhelm the man, so I decided to start with a simple one. "So, while you've been attending the Private Equity Summit, what is the rest of the family up to?"

"I imagine that Catherine and Heather are probably shopping or at a spa," he chuckled.

"And what about Matt and Brian?"

"Why don't you ask them yourself?"

"What?" I asked confused. "You mean at dinner tonight?"

"No…I mean now," he said gesturing toward a spot behind me.

I followed his gaze and froze as I saw them. The Cort brothers were coming toward us strutting like they were on the catwalk. It was only in the final seconds upon seeing my face that their stride lost some of its swagger.

Chapter 3: The Cort Brothers

When Heather asked me to come over to her house for a playdate, I was overjoyed, marking my calendar with a red Sharpie and counting down the days. I could hardly contain my excitement when the day finally arrived.

"Aw, this is brilliant. Thank you for inviting us into your lovely home," my mom said as she greeted Mrs. Cort for my *first* playdate with Heather.

We all lived in the small New England coastal town of Marblehead. Although we were geographically close - our worlds were far apart. Whereas, my family fit the typical stereotype for the suburban middle class with a good job, nice home, beautiful wife, and two kids. The Corts, with their incredible wealth and exquisite good looks, were like dream figures that seemed unreachable and untouchable. They lived in a massive oceanfront estate in the wealthiest part of town that was connected by the causeway and beach. The area was known as the "Neck" and it was an exclusive five-mile stretch of gorgeous waterfront houses and elite yacht clubs that offered spectacular views of the harbor, Atlantic Ocean, and the Boston skyline.

"Thank you, Mrs. Nottingham. When we originally found this house; it was a small beach cottage, but we fell in love with the view and over the years we've transformed it and reworked the entire floor plan. Would you like to join me for a coffee while the kids play and then I could give you a tour?"

"That would be grand Mrs. Cort, but please call me Maeve."

"Only if you call me Catherine," Mrs. Cort chuckled. "Are you Irish?"

"Why do you ask?"

"Well, you have a bit of an Irish accent when you talk."

"Yes," my mother nodded, "and Welsh."

"Ahh, I should have guessed with your natural Celtic beauty. Samantha has your same dark-haired good looks."

I rolled my eyes. Were they ever going to stop talking?

"Thank you and Heather clearly resembles you; she is a blonde beauty!"

"Are you trying to make me blush?" Mrs. Cort joked.

"I think, I've succeeded" My mother grinned. "Your boys are handsome devils too, but not as fair as you and Heather. Is the dark hair from your husband's side of the family?"

"Yes. Brian is a mix of the both of us, but Matt resembles my husband, Tom, so we often call him *Little Tom*."

"Well, I think we'll have our hands full when the kids are older, and they start to notice the opposite sex."

Mrs. Cort playfully covered her ears. "I don't even want to think about that!"

"Mom?" I yelped tugging at her skirt. Finally, she looked at me. "Sorry, Sam, you must be bored listening to us."

Mrs. Cort smiled sweetly at me. "Samantha, Heather is in the back yard with her brothers, and I know that she is eagerly awaiting your arrival. Do you want me to call her in or do you want to go outside?"

"That's ok Mrs. Cort, I'll go outside and find her." While my mom and Mrs. Cort bonded over coffee, which in later years became wine, I opened the glass door and walked onto an oceanfront deck that overlooked lush lawns and gardens that were the size of a soccer field. Because I was only six years old, I wasn't intimidated by my lavish surroundings; instead I was enchanted by the totally awesome swing set, tennis court, trampoline, and pool. Heather's backyard was better than a trip to the playground; it was almost as good as going to the amusement park.

I heard Heather call my name and I made my way across the yard toward a clump of trees at the furthest edge of the lawn, high above the sea.

"Hi!" I cheerfully greeted.

Three sets of the bluest eyes that I had ever seen stared at me, but then the boys quickly turned away and I saw that they were bickering about something.

Heather came over and gave me a huge hug. "Sam, I'm helping my brothers try to rescue an injured bird from that tree,"

Heather indicated by pointing to the highest branch of the tallest tree in her yard. Once that is done, we can go inside and make some beaded bracelets.

"Ok, but why are you guys bickering? I can just quickly climb up the tree and get the bird."

Suddenly, the bickering between the boys stopped and they turned in my direction. "That would be great!" said the younger boy with the floppy light brown hair, smiling at me in what could only be described as a winning smile.

"No, it's not great," said the older boy in a commanding tone to the younger one. Then he looked at me, and I caught my breath. He was the most handsome looking boy that I had ever seen in my life. "The robin is up too high, and it would be dangerous for you or anyone else to try to climb to that height."

"I know I can do it." I protested stubbornly.

"You want to climb the tree?" Heather shrieked, looking horrified. She was a girly girl and even at six years old, she had already started to paint and manicure her nails.

"Yeah, she can do it!" the younger boy spat out. "She weighs practically nothing."

"No one is climbing that high," said the older boy. "I'm going to get the pool net and see if I can capture the bird from one of the lower branches."

Once the older boy had walked away, the younger one turned to me. "The coast is clear Slim so if you want to climb, you better do it now before he comes back."

"Slim?" I questioned wrinkling my nose at the nickname as I headed to the tree and started to climb. *This should be a piece of cake!*

"I think Matt's right, come back." Heather yelled up to me sounding alarmed.

"Don't listen to her. You're doing great Slim!" the younger boy encouraged as I climbed the tree higher.

"If something happens to Samantha, this is all your fault Brian and I will tell MOM!" Heather threatened.

I was almost at the top, but then I looked down and realized that I was higher than I had ever been before. Holy Moly—this was a tall tree! I started to get nervous and my dirty hands became sweaty as I looked at the flimsy branch where the bird sat. Would it support my weight when I went on it? I wondered if I should have listened to the older boy. *I can do it. I can do it. I can do it.* I lightly climbed onto the flimsy branch and gently but firmly reached out to the injured bird.

SNAP.

I heard tree limbs breaking as I plummeted down. *OMG—I'm going to die!* But before I hit the ground, something grabbed me. I opened my eyes and found myself in the strong capable arms of the older boy who had climbed up the tree stopping my fall and saving my life. We even managed to save the Robin, which still sat securely in my hand.

***

My introduction to the Cort brothers that day was a fitting first impression. Brian, the younger one with floppy hair, was a cute and friendly kid. When given the opportunity, he would harass and tease me, tugging my hair and poking me until I begged for mercy. He had a happy demeanor and laughed out loud frequently. I liked him immediately.

Matt, the older one, was a really beautiful boy with an intense stare and I found it difficult to breathe around him. His manners were polite, but he barely showed any interest in me, so it took time to get to know him.

Where, Brian was simple and straightforward, Matt was complex and difficult to describe. The only thing I knew for certain was that Matt was destined for greatness. Yeah, I knew it sounded corny, but he had "it." You know, the elusive "it." Matt had those indefinable qualities that drew you in and commanded attention. He was going places and one knew that wherever he landed it would be in that ever-elusive top-dog spot.

Both were extreme competitors and were among the best athletes on the track and football teams. Matt was also an amazing sailor – winning many local and regional regattas, and Brian, a stellar snowboarder. While both had comparable athletic prowess and competitive streaks, their similarities ended there.

Matt was a natural born leader (class president and group leader for countless school and sports activities), and a diplomat with a golden tongue (debate club champion all four years of high school). He was a deep thinker and strategist, very charming and charismatic with an intensive magnetism.

Brian was Matt's polar opposite. He was a practical joker who loved to be the life of the party and he often went out of his way to be friendly and make people comfortable. He loved adventure, the great outdoors, and like Heather, he appreciated any excuse to socialize and party. Brian was an entertainer, who could always be counted on for fun and excitement.

Although I never admitted it to anyone, I had a crush on Matt from the very first moment I met him when he saved me from falling out of the tree. I valiantly hid my feelings for him, even with Heather. But sometimes I'd see him, and my face flushed, and my heart pounded, and I wondered if he knew how much I liked him.

My attraction to Matt was not for the obvious tall, dark, and handsome reasons. Sure, he was painfully handsome with thick, wavy brown hair, blue-grey eyes, and a sexy bad boy smile…yep he was the "Zeus" among the sex god family! If that wasn't enough to give a girl heart palpitation, he was a straight 'A' honors student with a perfect GPA, and he excelled at just about everything he tried. I won't lie and say that I wasn't fascinated by those traits, not to mention his rippling muscles and buns of steel. But when you pulled back the banana peel to look underneath, I really liked Matt, the person.

The problem with liking a Cort brother, especially the eldest Cort brother, was that they dazzled every girl living within a 50-mile radius. The Cort brothers were lady-killers and every girl in our school swooned when one of them walked by. I never stood a chance with Matt, or even with Brian for that matter, so I buried those feelings and became the next best thing…their "sister-like" best friend.

Chapter 4: The Boat Shack – June 2005

Breathing in the glorious sea air, Heather and I parked the car along the harbor and wandered up a narrow twisting street in the historic area of Marblehead, known as Old Town. As we approached our destination, I could hear the muffled lyrics of "Piano Man" by Billy Joel mixed with the sound of loud voices and laughter coming from inside.

The Boat Shack was a popular hangout. It remained modest, bordering on decrepit, despite some of the wealthy clientele who frequented it. I liked it, because it was comfy, like an old shoe, and it served truly epic fried seafood in its downstairs dining room. I had never been upstairs at the pub before, because you had to be twenty-one to get in, but it quickly earned the reputation as the best watering hole on the North Shore for its ample bar, cheap prices, and the biggest, strongest drinks around.

My face flushed as we approached the entrance where Skippy stood checking ID's. I knew that Heather was dead set on going in at this point, so I tried behaving like I belonged there. I just hoped she didn't get me in trouble.

"Hey girls!" Skippy greeted us with a big grin on his face. "Heather, are you going to introduce me to your friend?"

"Skippy, it's Samantha Nottingham. You know, Pete's sister." Heather said dryly, rolling her eyes at him.

"Wow…you've grown up," he said sounding embarrassed. "I didn't recognize you."

"Thanks," I muttered while looking at the ground.

"Pete and Brian are graduating high school, right?" Skippy asked directing the question at me.

"Yeah, it's this weekend." I commented

"What are those lucky dogs up to anyway?"

"Well, they're with friends in the Cape this week and after graduation they're going with Jackson Flynn and his family on an African Safari."

"Nice!" Skippy marveled. "Where are they going to school in the fall?"

"Brian is going to Brown and Pete will be a Yale Man!" I said with an amused grin.

"No shortage of brain power there!" Skippy smirked.

"Skippy!" Heather chirped. "The graduation party is this weekend and it's going to be one helluva a party!" She insinuated, dangling it out there like a carrot on a string.

"Is that an invitation?" He asked.

"You can come Skippy, but only if you let us upstairs," Heather flirted in her low and sexy voice.

"If I let you girls go inside, but you have to promise me no drinking, otherwise my man Matty will have my head. Is it a deal?"

"Scouts Honor," Heather said raising her hand in a salute.

"Hey Heather, before you ladies take off, where's the GQ model anyway? Is he home from Stanford yet?"

"Yes, Matt got home today, Skip."

"What?" I said joining the conversation. "Why didn't you say so when I asked you earlier?"

Heather looked at me with a smug grin. "Well, now you know Sammy!" Then she added with a smirk, "You'll see Matt when you sleep over tonight."

I almost squealed with delight, but instead I casually shrugged. "Great, I haven't seen him in a while." *Holy Cow! That was an understatement.* The previous summer Matt had not come home at all, because he had done an internship at Goldman Sachs in New York. Then he spent Thanksgiving with his roommate's family in California, and for Christmas my family and I went away skiing. After eighteen months apart, I would finally see him tonight!

***

My head was swimming from all the super-sized "big gulp" drinks we had consumed. I knew that we had promised Skippy that we wouldn't drink, but when preppy, waspy, and plaid twenty-two year old Tanner Harrington, who graduated a class above Matt, and his buddies Reed and Josh, sent us a round of drinks in the giant red tumblers, we decided it would be rude to refuse. Tanner looked like a poster child for one of those glossy Ralph Lauren advertisements. You know the ad I mean, with the perfect preppy family sailing on their yacht or frolicking on a white sandy beach, most likely shown against a backdrop of Nantucket or Newport, Rhode Island. Anyway, Heather persuaded me that there was no real harm in having just one drink. Soon after, Tanner, Reed, and Josh asked if they could join us, and before I knew it, several rounds later, we were hammered, and I was holding the edge of the table to keep myself from falling and passing out.

"Last Call!" yelled the bartender.

"What?" my head jerked up in surprise. *Hiccup.* "Is it late?"

"It's only eleven, but this fuddy-duddy town is lame," Reed complained.

"Yep, the joys of small towns. Talk about BORING, man," Josh chimed in disgusted. "It's only eleven and look how empty the bar is. What a joke."

"Well then, we will just have to make our own excitement," Tanner said smugly as he stood up. Then he raised his voice and tapped his glass, drawing the attention of the remaining bar patrons. "Tonight, I invite you all on my boat for a ride across the harbor for one last drink in Salem."

The neighboring city of Salem is located just across the harbor from Marblehead and is a short boat ride away. It's best known for Halloween, wicked witches and haunted happenings, but for locals, especially those single, and under the age of thirty, Salem is better known for bars that are open until 1am.

"Yippee!" Heather giggled putting down her phone and giving me a squeeze. "But we have to wait for Ryan," she slurred. "He should be here any minute."

"I'm not feeling so well," I said putting my head down on the table and shutting my eyes. "When Ryan gets here, let's have him drive us back to your house."

"What?" Tanner tightened his arm around me, and I looked up to find him very close to me. "You can't go home, beautiful, the night is still young."

"Yeah, Sammy. Don't be such a party pooper!" Heather pouted. "It's a perfect summer night for a boat ride. Just drink some water and you'll be fine."

I really wasn't feeling well, but I didn't bother to protest. "Okay," I slurred.

The warm air felt nice as we walked the short distance to the Boston Yacht Club where the Harrington's boat, Sailfish, was moored at the entrance of the harbor.

"Nice boat!" whistled a twenty-something year old girl (I think her name was Patty?) and her two friends, Ellie and Bridget, from the bar who had tagged along with us. You could tell that they liked Tanner, Reed, and Josh by the way they learned in and flirted with them. After seeing the size and grandeur of the boat, Patty whispered, rather loudly I might add, to Bridget, "Tanner's mine tonight and I'm so going to *do* him." Along with the three girls was a group of four guys who looked like overfed frat boys with bloated beer bellies. Rounding out our group was Heather, Ryan (who had shown up just as the bar was closing), and me, for a grand total of thirteen passengers aboard the Sailfish.

"What kind of boat is this, Tanner?" asked Patty as she looped her arm through his.

Before he could answer, I replied without thinking. "It's a 38-foot sloop with a 60-foot mast great for sailing and racing."

I could see Patty pouting, while I saw Tanner appreciatively look me over. "How do you know so much about boats?" he inquired.

Heather came up behind me and circled her arms affectionately around my neck. "Because Sammy here is an amazing sailor! One of the best."

"Oh yeah, where have you sailed?" Tanner asked with obvious interest.

"No where, really," I quietly said. "Just a couple of local junior races, no big deal."

Heather interrupted. "Don't let her fool you Tanner. She's really good."

Patty cleared her throat trying to redirect the conversation back to her and Tanner. "Why is your boat calling the Sailfish?"

"The sailfish is the world's fastest fish, and when we speed through the water, well, we live up to the name," Tanner said with a cocky grin and competitive sparkle in his eye.

"Ha! That's not true!" Heather blurted out.

Tanner made a face at her. "What?"

"Nothing," I replied quickly. "It's nothing."

"What's nothing?" Patty asked.

"Tanner has never been able to win against my brother and his crew on the Cortship," Heather replied with a shameless smile. "Matt is unbeatable."

Tanner glared at her. "Whatever. Matt will get his one day and I hope I'm the one that delivers it."

The conversation was dropped as the last of the group boarded the boat. We sailed into the warm summer night, and I started to feel better. The heat was still intense, but on the open ocean the wind picked up and carried a freshening breeze. We arrived at Pickering Wharf, a quaint harbor side village of shops and restaurants, in Salem around midnight and grabbed an outdoor table at Victoria Station, a waterfront restaurant and lounge. Everyone was over twenty-one, except Heather, Ryan and I, so they all drank while we kept them company. The guys kept pushing extra beers over to us, which I noticed Heather drank, but I decided to stick to water this time around as my borderline drunkenness had turned into a nice buzz and I wanted to keep it that way for the return trip back on the boat.

Before we left Salem, however, Reed and Josh did a final pit stop of the evening and when they returned to the boat, their arms were loaded with paper bags filled with alcohol and big red plastic cups.

"Did you get everything I asked for?" Tanner questioned.

"Of course, we did, man!" Josh laughed clapping Tanner on the back.

"Hey, everyone!" Tanner yelled. "Considering that we are on a boat we thought it only fitting to end the night with a Boat Race. Does everyone know how to play?"

A few people nodded and the bloated frat boys yelled "Hell Yes!"

"Well, for those who don't know how to play, I'll quickly go over the rules," Tanner said, staring intently at me. "I'm the referee and I'll divide everyone into equal teams. The first drinker on a team has to completely finish his or her drink of vodka or tequila and then put the empty cup on their head, before the next player on the team can go and so on and so on until the last player finishes. In a nutshell, the first team to finish their drinks wins the race. Got it everyone?"

"Why are you the referee?" Heather asked raising an eyebrow.

"Because I have to remain sober to drive the boat," he said conceitedly. "Any other questions?"

"It sounds fun, but make my drink a water," I mumbled.

Dumbfounded, everyone stared at me in shock and started to protest.

"That's not fair!" shrieked Patty. "What are you some kind of Puritan?"

"The whole point is that it's a drinking game, Samantha!" Josh cajoled. "You have to drink booze, not water."

"Samantha, we need you. If you don't drink, the teams will not be equal-sized," Reed pressed.

"Come on your big baby!" yelled Bridget.

"Don't call my friend a baby!" snapped Heather, clearly irritated while clinging onto Ryan to stand upright.

"Calm down everyone," said Tanner. "We bought cranberry juice, so anyone who doesn't want to drink the vodka straight can have a mixed drink with less alcohol. How does that sound? Samantha?"

I felt everyone staring at me. I sighed, folding my arms over my chest until I caved into the peer pressure. "Fine," I agreed, but even I could hear the strain in my voice from being forced to drink and play the stupid game. It was going to be a long night.

When we finally made it back to Marblehead after three rounds of Boat Race, I was officially wasted and so was Heather. We got off the boat, both laughing, with Ryan, Tanner and Patty following closely behind us. Tanner looked like he wanted to brush off Patty, but she continued to cling to him like Velcro. The bloated frat boys waved farewell, walking in the opposite direction from us and Bridget and Ellie were making out with Reed and Josh in front of the boat pier. Heather was staggering and leaning on me as we walked to her car. I tripped over something causing us both to fall and we doubled over in uncontrollable giggles. "Oops," I laughed as we hit the ground.

Ryan reached out and plucked Heather off the ground. "Ouch," she gasped, staggering a bit to get her balance.

A wave of dizziness hit me, and I closed my eyes. When I reopened them, my feet were suddenly off the ground. Tanner picked me up and threw me over his shoulder while Patty glared at me. "What are you doing?" I sputtered. "Put me down!" Tanner ignored me and walked a short distance until he reached a sidewalk bench where he deposited me. Ryan followed suit and placed Heather next to me on the bench that was a short distance from her car.

"Listen, you guys clearly cannot drive home, so why don't you crash at my place?" Tanner suggested while Patty looked on with a sour expression.

"Won't your parents be pissed?" Ryan asked.

"Parents?" Tanner asked quizzically. "I just graduated college, man. I don't live with them."

"Where do you live?" Patty asked eagerly.

"My place is less than a five-minute walk," Tanner indicated, pointing in the direction of the Boston Yacht Club where we had just walked from when he parked his boat. "It's a condo on the water next to the yacht club."

"Nice bro!" Ryan said with admiration. "So, you're living back here permanently?"

"Well, now that I'm home from college, my dad expects me to go into the family boat building business," admitted Tanner with a casual shrug. "I think the condo was a bribe to make me stay here."

Heather gave me a look of warning. "Thanks for the sleep over invitation Tanner," Heather chimed in with her overly false sweet voice, "but we want to go home. Don't *we* Sam?"

"Yes, let's go home," I agreed, rubbing my throbbing head and stomach.

"I'm okay to drive," Ryan spoke up. "Heather, give me your keys?"

I watched as she searched for her bag, and the corners of her mouth turned down. "Shit."

"What's wrong?" I asked panicked.

"I think I left my bag with my keys, phone, and wallet either on Tanner's boat or at the Boat Shack or Victoria Station."

Tanner smirked. "I guess it's settled. You can all sleep at my place."

"Not so fast," Heather slurred. "Sam, give me your phone."

"Sure." I handed her my phone and watched her dial.

"Matt!" she gushed. Pause. "Sorry, I know it's almost three in the morning." Pause. "No, nothing is wrong, but I lost my car keys and we need a ride home." She laughed nervously. Long silence. "I am not drunk." Pause "Yes, we umm…drank a little." She giggled. Long silence. "Yes, Sam is with me and so is Ryan." Pause. "Yes, they are both fine." She rolled her eyes and smirked. Pause. "Ok. My car is near the Boat Shack at the bottom of the hill. We will meet you there once we look for my purse on Tanner's boat." Pause. "Yes, Tanner Harrington." Long silence. "Stop yelling at me," she slurred. Pause. "Ok…see you soon," she slurred again.

Heather handed me back my phone. "Matt is coming to get us. He should be here soon." Then, she turned her head to Tanner. "While we're waiting, do you mind if Ryan, Sam, and I check your boat for my purse?"

"Go ahead," he said stiffly looking unhappy at the turn of events. "Actually, let's all head over there so that Patty can find her friends."

They all turned to leave, but I lingered on the bench.

"Are you coming Sammy? Hey, you don't look so good." Heather said touching my face and rubbing my back tenderly."

I had a sudden bout of nausea, and another wave of dizziness. "I'll just stay here and wait for Matt," I mumbled incoherently.

Before anyone could answer, Tanner took command of the situation and quickly sat next to me on the bench barking out random orders to everyone. "I'll wait with Samantha! You guys GO check the boat! Now!"

"Don't order me around, Tanner Harrington!" Heather hissed putting her hands on her hips. I could tell she was ready to let him have it, but before she could reprimand him, Ryan grabbed her and started moving her in the direction of the boat. "Come on, we don't have time to argue. What color is your purse?" Heather hesitated for a moment and turned to me and shouted. "Sam, we will be back in 10!" Then she walked away with Ryan toward the boat.

Just when I thought it would finally be quiet, Patty came up close to Tanner on the bench. "But Tanner," Patty complained in her nasally voice. "I wanted to hang with you."

"That's sweet Patty, but why don't you go find your friends and I'll be along shortly to check in with everyone and wrap up the night."

"Fine," she huffed turning to leave and angrily stomping away trailing behind Heather and Ryan.

When they were out of hearing distance, Tanner turned toward me and cringed, shaking his head. "I thought Patty would never leave me alone tonight. Thank god she finally got the hint...Yuck!"

"S-she likes you," I stuttered in my alcoholic haze.

"Well, I don't like her," he said distastefully, shaking his head like he was repulsed at the very idea of her. Then he turned his head to me, and slowly slid his hand down my arms and over my back. "How are you feeling, beautiful?"

"N-not so good," I murmured.

"Well you don't look sick. In fact, you look like a model that just got off the runway. I haven't been able to take my eyes off you all night. You're fucking beautiful!" Then he surprised the hell out of me and before I knew it, I could feel his lips on mine. The kiss felt nice and without thinking about it, I shifted my body closer to him and deepened the kiss.

Suddenly he grabbed my ass and lifted me onto his lap pressing me against his erection and I panicked. "Please stop, Tanner."

"Why? What's wrong beautiful?"

I tried to focus to tell him to stop, but I bit my lip unable to form a coherent thought. *Whoa, I was drunk!*

Looking into my eyes, he stroked a piece of hair aside and trailed kisses down my neck, roughly sucking and biting at my flesh. "Why don't you come back to my place and you can wash up and have some water and Advil. You'll feel better in no time."

"N-no thanks," I slurred. "Matt will be here any minute."

"Are you dating him?" Tanner suddenly asked.

"Matt? N-no, we're just friends."

"Good," Tanner whispered smugly in my ear. He pressed his hands on either side of me and kissed me quickly again. Then he slid his hand under my shorts making me uncomfortable. "Please come back to my place?"

When I answered, I tried very hard *not* to slur my words. "I don't do booty calls, Tanner."

"Are you sure?" He chuckled and grabbed my ass. "You have such a hot body."

"Yeah, I'm fuckin' sure!" I snapped, trying to push him away. "Now let go of me Tanner."

"You heard the lady! Get the hell away from her, before I smash that arrogant grin off your face!"

My head shot up in surprise. I would recognize that deep masculine voice anywhere and I felt my stomach flutter. Then I saw him come into view, and it felt like my heart was going to explode; there Matt stood, sleep deprived and strikingly handsome. I watched with discomfort, biting my lip, as a scowl formed on his perfect face as he took in the sight of me drunk, sitting on Tanner's lap. Matt was angry.

He stormed over to where Tanner and I sat on the bench. "Come on Sam, it's time to go," he said with authority, wrapping his huge hands around my waist, and pulling me off Tanner's lap, until I stood next to him. He held me upright looking concerned. "Are you ok?" he whispered in my ear.

"I just want to go home," I murmured quietly, leaning against Matt, as I ambled to his car.

"Not so fast, Cort!" Tanner screamed. "I should kick your ass!"

Matt ignored him as he helped me get into his car. "If you feel like you're going to be sick, keep your head out the window…ok Sam?"

I nodded my head, but then I shrieked, "Watch Out Matt!" as I saw Tanner come up behind Matt and push him roughly against the car. Tanner was about to hit Matt in the face, when Matt rolled to the right avoiding Tanner's fist. The next thing I knew, Matt punched Tanner in the stomach, and then again in his face, knocking Tanner on his ass. Tanner got up, but stumbled, falling backwards. He was livid, screaming and waving his hands wildly. "I'm going to kill you, Cort!" he thundered.

"Bring it on, Tanner! Because you fight, the way you sail, like an egotistical, dimwitted, powder puff!" Matt goaded, egging Tanner on.

Tanner took the bait, stalking over to Matt in a fit of rage, his knuckles white, and his hands curled into fists. But before Tanner could try to throw another punch, I heard Heather scream, and then Ryan came and stood between the guys breaking up the fight.

"It's time for everyone to go home," Ryan gently, but firmly said. "Now."

There was a prolonged moment of unease while Tanner and Matt took another minute to glare at each other. Finally, Ryan turned to Tanner, arching an eyebrow at him. "Hey man, Patty and the rest of the group are waiting for you. Come on Tanner, the party's over."

"Fine. I'm going." Tanner muttered.

Matt kept his eyes on Tanner while he said this and then he smirked. "Bye Tanner." He paused before gleefully adding, "As always it's been a real pleasure to knock you on your ass."

As Tanner turned to go, he roughly bumped Matt's shoulder. "This isn't over," he said through gritted teeth. Then he called out sweetly to me. "Until later, beautiful," and he was gone.

Chapter 5: An Awkward Reunion – May 2013

I watched panic-stricken, as the Cort brothers made their way over to where Mr. Cort and I stood. It seemed like everything was in slow motion. *Oh God.* I wished I could slip away, but it was too late. They had spotted me and there was nowhere to escape. "It's Sam!" I heard Brian say to Matt only seconds before they reached us. Determined to regain my composure, I took a large gulp of air reminding myself to *breathe in, breathe out.* I smiled calmly, straightening my back and lifting my chin to meet their gaze. *I could do this! After all, eight years had passed.*

"Slim!" Brian's deep voice boomed over the sea of people in the reception area. Before I could react, he took me in his arms and twirled me around like a giddy schoolboy. "Sam, I can't believe it's really you!"

"Put me down you big oaf!"

He frowned. "Sorry. I think I messed up your hair." He set me down and we stood in silence for a few moments, just grinning at each other. Brian was such a cheery guy that I immediately felt foolish for my irrational panic at seeing him again.

"How the heck are you Brian?"

Brian laughed and shook his head with a big grin on his face "A lot better now!" he chuckled. "To think, I didn't even want to come to this boring conference, and now I'm so happy that I did."

"Ahem." Matt cleared his throat to speak. "Yes, Brian, I would agree that the Private Equity Summit just got a whole lot more interesting." My back was to him, but there was a powerful intensity to his voice that made me want to turn around, so I did.

The electricity was palpable the moment our gazes locked, and my heart rate increased. He looked good. Really, really ridiculously good looking. And then I realized that I was staring at him for a moment longer then what was politely acceptable.

"How are you Matt?" I asked casually, betraying none of my inner turmoil.

"It's good to see you, Sam." The expression on Matt's face was neutral and unreadable, but his voice held such sincerity, that I wanted to believe him. He knitted his brow and tilted his chin up slightly, wordlessly asking me something that I didn't understand. I stood there like a confused idiot trying to decipher his meaning, when he suddenly grinned, a disarming smile. Then he reached confidently across me, leaned in smoothly, and kissed my cheek. He was charming in that way that couldn't be taught or learned, and I couldn't deny that I'd always found it attractive.

Before I could delve deeper into my psychoanalysis of Matt or how it felt to see him again, Mr. Cort spoke. "Sam is going to join us for dinner tonight boys. Isn't that right Sam?" he asked quirking up an eyebrow.

"Yes, just tell me where and when Mr. Cort, and I promise I'll be there."

"We're staying at the Mandarin adjacent to Hyde Park, so why don't you meet us at Bar Boulud at 8:00?"

"That sounds great!" I replied. "I'm really excited to see Heather tonight. Maybe you shouldn't tell her that I'm coming to dinner and we could surprise her?"

"Ha!" Brian said eagerly. "That's a great idea! She is going to have a heart attack when she sees you."

"More reason to do it then," I smiled mischievously.

"Are your parents still living in London?" Mr. Cort inquired. "Could they join us for dinner?"

"I wish they could join us, but my dad is on a business trip to Switzerland and my mom went with him. They won't be back in London until Friday and I know that they will be very disappointed that they missed you guys. How long are you staying?"

"We fly out Thursday," replied Mr. Cort. "What about you Sam? I heard Vijay say that your internship is ending and that you are coming back to America. When? What have you been up to since we last saw you and what are your plans moving forward?"

"Wow, that's a loaded question," I mumbled. "I don't want to bore you all."

"You won't bore us," Matt spoke up, his face intense and inquisitive. "What have you been up to for the last eight years? We *really* want to know."

Crap.

They all stood staring at me, patiently waiting for me to answer.

"C'mon Sam, spill?" Brian said.

Double crap.

I froze, staring at my damn shoes for what felt like minutes. The men hovered around me, and I bit my lip and grimaced. I hated being the center of attention and was still reeling from this unexpected reunion with them. "Well, that's a lot of information to cover. How about I tell you at dinner tonight?"

"No way, Sam, because Heather is going to monopolize you all night long and you know it!" Brian pleaded. "Come on, tell us what's going on."

"Um, ok. Well, you might remember that my dad left his professorship at MIT to take on a new position at the University of Cambridge?" They all nodded their consensus, urging me to continue. "After my high school graduation, we moved to London and I really loved it, so I decided to forgo Stanford, and I attended Cambridge instead.

Matt jerked his head up, a slight grimace appearing on his handsome face. "You didn't end up going to Stanford?"

My face reddened, because I knew what he was thinking. He thought I didn't go to Stanford, because of him. "Um-no," I stuttered.

Mr. Cort coughed. "Cambridge is one of the best in the world. It's just as good as Stanford."

"Thanks Mr. Cort," I replied with a fond smile. "It was a great experience and I got to go tuition free, because of my dad."

"Tuition free! That's always a great perk!" piped up Brian.

"So, have you been in London this whole time?" Matt asked, his eyes questioning, urging me forward.

"No, after college, I went to New York. I got my MBA at New York University."

"Another excellent program," Mr. Cort praised. "Any specific specializations?"

"Yes, taxation and international law."

"Nice Sammy!" cheered Brian. "You always were a brain just like Matty"

"I thought you went to Brown and UCLA, Brian?"

"Your point, Sam?" Brian volleyed back to me.

"Not exactly minor league education, Brian. Is it?" I smirked.

"I guess, but it's not the top in the world like Stanford or Harvard," Brian said, his tone a mixture of teasing and bitterness. "Is it, Matt?"

"Are we going to do this again?" Matt asked Brian, the tension thick between them.

"Nah, you know I'm joking, Matt, I just like to rile you up."

"Well, you are *irritatingly* good at it!" Matt joked, softening the mood.

It was nice to hear them bicker again. It reminded me of old times, before everything got so screwed up. I cringed remembering that last year together and the animosity between them, because of me. It was not a fond memory. I shook my head slightly, trying to clear it. "So, did you go to Harvard then?" I asked Matt directly. "When?"

He nodded. "After Stanford, I came home and did my MBA at Harvard while joining the Cort Group full-time."

"O-oh," was all I said.

"Samantha, have you been working with Vijay since graduating NYU?" Mr. Cort suddenly asked.

"Yes, Vijay knows my dad and he is an expert in virtual currencies, which was the topic of my master's thesis. I've been doing an internship with him at the London School of Business and at CVC Partners."

"Impressive Samantha" Mr. Cort said. "CVC is one of the top private equity firms. I heard Vijay say that you were moving back to America and job hunting, where and when?"

"Yes, I move next week. I'll be staying with my brother, Peter, in New York until I find a job and a place of my own. I'm fairly optimistic about the job hunt as I already have a few good interviews lined up."

"Pete's in New York!" Brian's face lit up. "How is my old buddy?"

"Really good. I'll give you his contact info so that you guys can catch up."

"That would be great, Sam!"

"Listen Samantha…" Mr. Cort began. "I don't know what type of job interviews you have lined up, but I think you should come work for us instead."

"What?" I asked, not hiding the shock in my voice. "You mean in Boston? What would I be doing?"

"For one, you're like a family member, and the Cort Group, first and foremost, is a family business. Depending on what you want to do, you could come work for us in Boston or in our New York office."

"When did you open a New York office?" I asked, trying to organize my thoughts. I was bombarded with so many mixed emotions, that I really needed some time to process how I was feeling about this sudden turn of events.

The sound of a chime ringing broke through the silence indicating that the next round of seminars would begin in five minutes. I frowned, more confused than ever. Meanwhile, Mr. Cort cleared his throat to speak, forcing me away from my random thoughts and bringing me back to the present conversation. "Samantha, we have to attend the next seminar so let's discuss this in greater detail tonight. Hopefully, by the end of the evening I will have persuaded you to join our firm. How does that sound?"

I had nothing coherent to say, so I nodded my head and mumbled my agreement. We said our goodbyes and as they walked away, Matt turned to me and smiled, a smile that was mischievous, wise, and knowing at the same time. It was a smile that I had often tried to forget over the last eight years. But his damn little smile was the most beautiful smile that I had ever seen, and despite my best efforts, it was unforgettable and heart breaking, like the man himself.

Chapter 6: Hangover: The Morning After – June 2005

"I'm dying!" I screeched putting my head back on the pillow and shutting my eyes. It felt like someone had thrown a sizable rock at my head and the room was spinning. After several long minutes, I tried to open my eyes again, this time waiting for the fuzzy haze to lift. Slowly, miraculously the room came into focus giving me the newfound courage to try to sit up. "Fuuuck. My head hurts." Eventually I let my legs fall slowly off the edge of the bed and I pulled myself up. My stomach felt like someone had burned a hole in it and in that moment, I swore that I would never drink again.

I really didn't want to get out of bed, but I had to go to the bathroom, so I had no choice. That's when I noticed the water and aspirin on the bedside table, and I smiled with relief. I swallowed the aspirin quickly and walked toward the guest bathroom, awkwardly stumbling along the way. When I looked in the mirror, I was horrified by my reflection. Smudged mascara raccoon eyes looked back at me and revealed hair like a bird's nest, and love bites down my neck. But what really disturbed me was that I was half naked wearing only a skimpy white cotton thong and a rumpled man's polo shirt, and then it hit me, every awful, embarrassing moment from the night before came flooding back and I wanted the ground to swallow me up.

I painfully recalled the evening at the Boat Shack, and the stupid drinking game on Tanner's boat, followed by the conceited son of a bitch making a pass at me, and then the nasty fight that broke out between Matt and him. I involuntarily shuddered when I thought about Heather throwing up in the back seat of Matt's car on the drive home and the stench of the vomit hitting me hard. I remembered how my stomach churned and turned over at the aroma, and how I lost it just as Matt pulled into the Corts' driveway. At least, I didn't throw up in his car, like Heather did. She was going to be on his *shitlist* forever for that one. Matt's poor car. Anyway, I did the next best embarrassing thing and I vomited all over the Corts' driveway, repeatedly. Oh, what a horrid sight it must have been for Matt and Ryan to witness me hurling.

But those activities, while admittedly embarrassing, were nothing, compared to what happened between Matt and I later that same night. Oh My God! I wanted a truck to hit me now. How would I ever face him again? I'd had more sexual fantasies about Matt than I could count, but nothing could have prepared me for the humiliation of last night. Never could I have imagined, not even in my wildest dreams, the stupid drunken things that I had said (and did) to him last night. How could I have gotten so drunk? Shit. I was mortified beyond belief!

The shower felt divine and I almost felt human again. I was hungry and I wanted to go downstairs, but I was a coward and I was terrified of running into Matt, so I hid in the guest room for longer than I should. What would I say to him? *Sorry Matt for the extremely drunk kiss and for showing you my tits?* Or maybe I should say nothing and pretend that I didn't remember doing it. *Yes, that could work ... I could say nothing and feign ignorance over my drunken and disorderly conduct.* If he didn't bring it up, neither would I. With a new steely resolve, I made my way downstairs.

Ryan was sitting at the kitchen table hunched over a glass of water, and he looked like shit. "Morning," he mumbled.

"I think it's officially afternoon," I mumbled back. "Where is everyone?"

"Mr. Cort went to work early this morning, and Mrs. Cort went to some charity thing. Heather is still passed out in bed, and Matt went to get his car detailed."

"Matt's poor car, he must be pissed. Did Mr. or Mrs. Cort have a clue as to what happened last night?" I asked fearfully.

"Nah, Matt did a good job covering up everything and we hosed off the driveway and cleaned up his car the best we could."

"Does his car stink?" I asked worried.

"Well, it's not exactly smelling like roses!" Ryan chuckled. "We left the windows opened all night and hopefully, the detailing will help."

"Heather is so dead!" I exclaimed. "He loved that car."

"Yup, it's going to take her a long time to live it down. That's for sure!" Ryan agreed.

Just then I heard the garage door open and a few minutes later Matt walked in. "Good afternoon," he chuckled as he turned on the coffee maker. How's the hangover?"

"You don't have to sound so chipper about it," Ryan answered warily.

"You play, you pay!" Matt announced jovially. I had the distinct feeling that he was enjoying our suffering. Then he stopped in front of me, a slightly tense look on his face. "What about you, Sam?"

I poured cheerios and milk into a bowl. "I'll survive," I said awkwardly, trying to avoid his eyes as I took a bite of my cereal. He moved away then and busied himself with making coffee. When he wasn't looking, I stole a quick glance at him, but his expression was void of emotion, so I had no idea what he was thinking.

"My poor aching head," Heather announced, rather dramatically I might add, as she entered the kitchen. A shocked smile graced my face when I realized that she was wearing sweatpants and no make-up. Heather always looked the picture of perfection, so this was a rare occasion to say the least.

Matt came over with mugs of coffee for everyone. "Now that you are all here, it's time we had a little talk."

"Do we have to do this *now* Matt?" Heather whined in her little girl voice. "My head is killing."

"Yes – we do." he answered coolly.

"Fine Matt," Heather said looking up at him. "If you are going to scream at us, then let's just get it over with."

He sighed and his jaw was clenched. "What were you all thinking?" he asked, his tone irritated, but calm. "I'm not going to give you a lecture on underage drinking, because I get it, and we have all been there. But you must learn your limits, before something really bad happens. It's one thing to go out and get a little buzzed, but what you all did was totally idiotic and reckless. I repeat that bad things can happen, and you need to learn your limits." There was a slight pause, and then glancing in my direction, he added in a firm, angry voice. "I shudder to think what would have happened if I hadn't shown up when I did."

"Message received." Heather replied, sounding cranky. "Are we done?"

I'd never seen Matt so visibly mad with Heather before. "No, we're not done," he mimicked in a tight, irritated voice. "What were you thinking going on that Jackass's boat?"

"Matt, I know you think Tanner is a conceited, spoiled brat, but we were just hanging out." Heather tried to explain, shrugging her shoulder. "It was no big deal."

"No big deal?" he huffed. "Tanner and his womanizing friends went out of their way to get you and Sam drunk. If Ryan hadn't shown up, I'm sure Reed and Josh would have been all over you the way Tanner was all over Sam."

"Puh-lease Matt." Heather said rolling her eyes. "We can take care of ourselves."

"Sure, you can," he smirked. "You just keep telling yourselves that, because that's the funniest thing I've heard all day," Matt said in a self-righteous, condescending tone.

Heather was quiet for a few moments before speaking "I'm sorry," she reluctantly admitted.

"I don't want your apologies," he said looking at Heather and then at Ryan and me. "I just want you to be careful and use better judgment in the future, ok?"

"Ok," Heather said as she hugged him. "I'm sorry about your car."

"Don't worry, you'll pay for it," he smirked.

"Come on, let's go in the backyard and get some fresh air," Heather said to no one in particular.

"You and Ryan go ahead." Matt answered for the both of us, his voice serious when he spoke. "Sam and I are going to catch up for a bit. We will be there soon."

Heather gave us a surprised look, flickering her eyes between us. Then she got up to leave with Ryan, an amused expression on her face. "O-okay, we will see you later."

I wanted to beg Heather not to leave, but I knew that I couldn't shun away from this and that I would have to face Matt sooner or later. I had just hoped that it would be much later, like another century from now, but obviously Matt wasn't going along with my game plan. I took a long sip of my coffee and nervously pushed my cheerios in and out of the milk with my spoon. Matt didn't say a word and with each passing moment I grew more and more restless until I slowly raised my eyes to him. He was staring at me, his gaze intense, and my stomach fluttered. I was uneasy, but I decided to speak first. "I-I'm sorry M-Matt," I stuttered, anxious to get the apology over with.

"For what Sam?" he said in a husky voice as his eyes wandered over my face in a slow and deliberate fashion.

It was the second time today that I wished that the ground would swallow me up. "For…for…last night," I sputtered.

"Last night?" he said cocking an eyebrow, his gorgeous face breaking out into a delicious smirk. "That's a broad apology, would you care to elaborate, Sam, or are we going to dance around it all day?"

"Come on Matt, you're being a dick!" I balked darkly getting up from the table in marching away. "You know what I'm talking about."

Matt responded with a chuckle and I wanted to kick him. "I'm just horsing around with you Sam. Will you please come back to the table?"

I avoided his gaze, as I stalked back over to the table and sat down with a resounding thud. "I was stupid and drunk last night," I said, my words coming out in a jumbled rush. "I'm sorry Matt if I did anything to make you uncomfortable. I would die if this changed things between us." I laughed nervously. "Are we ok?"

He chuckled softly. "We're fine, Sam." I watched as he moved in closer to me, and whispered in my ear, "But I'll *never* think of you as my sister again!" Then he winked at me, grinning like a devil.

Without needing to look at a mirror, I was sure that I was probably blushing like crazy, and from that smirk on Matt's face, he was enjoying my discomfort just a little too much. *Cocky bastard.*

"By the way Sam," Matt said, his eyes drifting slowly over my body, "you can keep my shirt from last night."

I was so startled by his teasing that my mouth fell open, but I quickly recovered and punched him in the arm. Before long we were both laughing uncontrollably like children, so much so that it took several minutes before we could regain our composure and breath normally again.

"Do you want to go outside?" I asked, getting up, and putting my cereal bowl and coffee mug into the dishwasher.

"Before we do that, I have something I'd like to discuss with you first," he replied, suddenly serious. "Actually, two things."

The jovial atmosphere in the kitchen from only a few minutes before had suddenly shifted and I was weary and on edge again. My voice was tentative when I responded to him. "Alright Matt, what is it?"

He gave me a strange look. "So, you and Brian?" he tentatively began, his unspoken question hanging between us.

"What about Brian and me?" I asked self-consciously, not quite sure what he was insinuating.

"What's going on there?" he asked, raising an eyebrow as he stared at me, the curiosity clearly evident on his face.

"What do you mean?" I asked feigning innocence. "We're friends."

"Oh really, just friends?" he challenged. "Does Brian know that?"

"Yes, we *are* friends!" I replied. "Why? What have you heard?"

"I bet you would like to know!" he teased slowly, and I flushed. I started moving around the room, busying myself with this and that. Finally, I crossed to the other side of the kitchen and looked out the window to admire the ocean view. "I'm still waiting," he said playfully, coming up behind me, and gently turning me around to face him.

"Err…Brian is great, but he's practically like family," I said, desperately hoping that Matt dropped it, because I didn't want to discuss it further.

"Family, huh?" he asked amused, watching me closely. "So, do you make it a habit to kiss all your family members?"

I rolled my eyes. "You really are a smug bastard Matt. Do you know that?"

He smirked. "Well, thank you."

"It's not a compliment!"

He shrugged. "Did you know that Brian likes you?"

"Friends usually like each other." I laughed nervously. "What's your point?"

"Sam, stopping acting obnoxious, because you know exactly what I mean."

"Can we please just drop it?"

He stared at me for a long time, evidently debating if he should push it further. Finally, he nodded his agreement, apparently satisfied with my answer. "Since you're so reluctant to discuss Brian and what happened between you two at Prom," he smirked, "I'll let you dodge the bullet, at least for now, Sam."

"Gee, thanks Matt." I said sarcastically. I was about ready to step away and go outside when he took my elbow. "Not so fast Sam. We still have one more topic that I wanted to discuss," he paused for a moment, and then he cleared his throat, a grave look suddenly appeared on his face, "Tanner Harrington."

Chapter 7: Family Dinner in London – May 2013

I arrived at the Mandarin Oriental, Hyde Park at 7:45 pm and went to the bathroom to fix my lip-gloss and brush my long, dark hair out of the bun that it had been in all day. For the umpteenth time, I assessed myself critically in the mirror and wondered if the slit on my dress was too high? *Was I overdressed? Was it to provocative? Too revealing?* I had swapped the suit that I had worn during the conference for a seriously sexy, curve-enhancing wraparound dress. Usually I oozed confidence and style when I wore the scarlet dress, but tonight nothing could squelch my nerves. I was completely overwrought about sharing a meal with The Cort family and what it might lead too.

Promptly, I made my way over to Bar Boulud at 8:00 p.m. The chic bistro was packed for a Tuesday evening and I had to crane my head over the guys in suits to get a glimpse of the zinc-topped bar. The bar was bursting at the seams, so it took me a few minutes to spot them. Heather and Mrs. Cort were sitting at the bar facing away from me, while Brian and Mr.

Cort stood opposite them. I did not see Matt, and for a pitiful moment my heart dropped. *Was he not joining us for dinner?* I started to fret and realized that I was letting him get under my skin again, eight years later. I quickly rallied, giving myself a pep talk. *You can do this!*

As I walked over to the bar, Brian and Mr. Cort caught sight of me and smiled appreciatively, watching until I came to a full stop at the rear of Heather and Mrs. Cort. Wrapping my arms around them in a hug from behind, I yelled, "Surprise!"

Startled, Heather spit out what she was drinking. Turning to me, she laughed, and yelped out in surprise, "Oh my god." Pause. She screeched louder. "I can't believe it's really you!" Then she began to cry, and we hugged for an absurdly long time. Then the whole 'hug, kiss, cry' was repeated with Mrs. Cort, until the men finally cleared their throats to regain our attention.

"Samantha, you are so beautiful and grown up," Mrs. Cort said wiping the tears from her eyes. "How long has it been?"

"Too long." I said, choking back tears. "How have you been?"

"We have been good dear, but we've missed you," she said good-naturedly. Then she turned to her husband and son, "were you in on this?"

"Yes, we ran into Sam at the Private Equity Summit this afternoon and rather than tell you about it, we decided on a pre-dinner surprise," Mr. Cort replied with a devious chuckle.

"I can't believe you kept it a secret!" Heather said excitedly. "Well, we have so much catching up to do; so get ready for at least fifty questions!" Then she looked down at her watch and sighed. "Where is Matt? It would be nice to be seated for dinner once before midnight."

"He will be here any minute," Mr. Cort replied. "He had to deal with an urgent business matter from the New York office and it really could *not* wait."

Heather rolled her eyes. "It's always urgent."

"If you are hungry," Brian offered, "I could have them seat us now?"

"Don't bother yet, Brian. Here he comes now." Mrs. Cort said, waving Matt over, while scrutinizing my face. I got the uncomfortable feeling that she was studying me for a reaction to make sure that I wouldn't crumple like a doll or run away, which was my previous M.O. for the last eight years.

Aware of Mrs. Cort looking, I forced a smile on my face and calmly and casually looked at the entrance where Matt was standing. I was shocked to find him staring at me, with a slow, sexy smile on his face. He walked gracefully over to meet us and apologized profusely for being late. I made no effort to speak but I couldn't deny that I was pleased to see him.

"Everything ok, son?"

"Yes, everything is fine, dad."

As Matt talked business with his dad and Brian, I took the time to study the trio. Mr. Cort was now in his late fifties and graying at the temples, but he was still a handsome devil like his sons. All three men were tall, lean and muscular. Matt resembled his father the most and they shared the same chiseled features that reminded me of a Greek god. They also radiated the same vigor and a sense of purpose. Brian on the other hand, with his sunny disposition and "cute" boy-next-door good looks, seemed less intimidating than his male-counterparts. He was by far the most relaxed and laid-back of the three men. At one point, Matt caught me looking and gave me a half-smile. I thought he looked tired and tense, and I wondered what his life was like now. Matt had always worked and played hard, and I imagined over the years that, had only increased with his job responsibilities.

Before meeting with the Corts for dinner, I had taken the time to research the Cort Group, especially since Mr. Cort had offered me a job. Mr. Cort led the advisory and private investment management firm as Chairman and CEO from the Boston headquarters. Matt was President, and head of the New York office, where I assumed, he lived, and Brian was VP of Business Development straddling both locations, thus I wasn't sure where he called home. The Cort Group remained privately owned and independent, with over $12 billion in assets under management.

The Boston office had a staff of about 60 employees and dealt primarily with serving the interests of high net-worth individuals, families, and small institutions.

The New York office had opened four years ago; originally with 18 employees and was now up to 40. In a recent *Forbes* magazine article about "The Top 50 Wealth Managers" the Cort Group was cited as Number 3 as the fastest growing client asset management and advisory firms.

I knew if I joined the Cort Group I would learn a lot, but the question was could I have a relationship with Brian and Matt again, and what would it be like working with them on a daily basis? I was all over the map with my feelings about what to do.

We were told that our table was ready for dinner and as I passed by Matt, he gently touched my elbow and spoke in a low voice that only I could hear. "You look beautiful, absolutely stunning, Sam, and I love the dress."

My cheeks reddened from his compliment. "Thank you," I murmured hastily as we carefully made our way to the dinner table. I hated that even after so much time had passed, one touch or compliment from Matt could still make my heart go pitter-patter.

After walking through a wine cellar, we were seated in the main dining room at a long wooden oblong table with views of the lively open kitchen and charcuterie counter. I was seated next to Heather, Brian and Matt opposite us, and Mr. and Mrs. Cort were seated on each end.

While Matt ordered bottles of burgundy for the table, and Brian recounted a client story to his father, I started to fill in Heather and Mrs. Cort on the missing eight years.

"Did you say that you're moving to New York next week?" Heather shrieked excitedly. "You should move in with me!"

The table had gotten quiet, as all eyes and ears were now focused on Heather and me. "Thanks, but I'm going to live with my brother, Pete, for the time being. When did you move to

New York?" I asked surprised. "I thought you were living in Los Angeles?"

"Sam, didn't you read any of my emails or texts?" I moved to New York over a year ago when I got the job as a fashion buyer for Barneys.

"Congratulations Heather! It sounds like your dream job; but what email? I haven't received any communications from you in over three years?"

"That's not true," Heather replied haughtily. "In fact, you were the one that blew me off."

"Well, I didn't get anything," I replied defensively. "What email address and phone number did you send it to?"

Heather shoved her iPhone in my face. "Is your contact information correct?"

"No way! This information has been out of date for years."

"Oh, it is?" she reluctantly drew her phone away from my face. "Well, if you would be a normal person and use social media like everyone else on the planet, it would be much easier to keep in touch."

"Just because I don't have time for Facebook, doesn't make me abnormal. Anyway, I *do* use social media occasionally," I said, shrugging.

"Ha! I beg to differ," she snorted, handing me her phone. "Could you enter your updated info, so we don't lose touch again?"

"Definitely."

As I entered my new contact info into Heather's phone, Brian handed me his phone next. "Not so fast, I want your digits too. Also, give me Pete's?"

Brian's request momentarily threw me off, but I quickly recovered and took his phone from him. "Um, ok."

"Stop." Matt suddenly ordered. I looked up surprised, as did everyone else at the table. "Sorry, I didn't mean to startle anyone, but we all want your contact information, so to save you from typing, I thought Heather could just send it along to everyone."

"Oh, that makes sense," I mumbled in agreement, slightly flustered to have them all in my life again.

By the time the first course was served, which included an amazing assortment of cheeses, pates, four kinds of sausages, and salads, Mr. Cort turned to me and said, "So Sam, let's discuss your potential role in the Cort Group." He described in detail the Cort Group training program and what to expect, while I listened politely and said nothing. It was only when my main course of *Aioli*, a classic French dish of cod poached in olive oil arrived, that Heather piped in, "Enough Dad. Are you trying to bore her to death?"

He laughed warmly. "Well, that's enough about it for now. Sorry for monopolizing you Sam." And just like that he started to eat his *coq au vin*. I felt a mild sense of relief that the business talk was suspended, at least for now, as I was still very much undecided about what I wanted to do.

A moment later, Heather recounted to my delight and horror, a run in with a former classmate of ours who she was convinced had made a pass at her.

Within minutes, the table broke out into laughter, followed by good-humored conversation for the rest of the evening. Happy memories of countless good times like these came flooding back and it made me really sad that I'd missed so much time. In that moment, I realized just how much I'd lost by losing touch with them, and how happy I was to be part of it again. Heather, Matt, and Brian, for better or worse, were probably the best friendships that I'd ever had. And I'd missed them so damn much.

So, at one point during the meal, when Brian turned to me and offered me a bite of his steak *frites* with Black Peppercorn Sauce, I nodded and leaned in, without really thinking twice about it. Brian fed it to me, but some sauce dropped on my chin. He laughed and started wiping my face with his own napkin. As he did this, his fingers lingered on my cheek for a fraction too long, and I was suddenly aware of his proximity, which made me tense up. He was definitely too close for comfort. I shifted away from him and pondered for what felt like the hundredth time that day if there was just too much history and hurt to be friends again, never mind potential colleagues.

I snuck a look at Matt out of the corner of my eye, and sure enough, I was met with a look of reproach. I frowned at Matt, but said nothing, and luckily no one else seemed to notice our frosty exchange. When dinner was finally winding down and the topic of me joining the Cort Group came up again – I was at a loss on what to do or how to respond.

I told them that I needed time to think about their offer. They were not pleased by my hesitancy, but granted me time to think, nonetheless. To appease them, we scheduled a meeting two weeks later in New York to discuss it further.

I was grateful for the opportunity and attention, but it also made me feel uneasy. I was torn between how to maintain my independence and still build our relationship with them at the same time. I loved them like my own family, and I very much wanted to reconnect with all of them, but when it came to Brian and Matt, my fight or flight reflex kicked into overdrive, and I overwhelmingly had the desire to sprint far away.

Heather, Matt and Brian walked me out while I hailed a cab home, and after saying our goodbyes, it occurred to me that nothing personal had really been discussed. Tonight, was only window dressing, casual, surface conversation. The real dialogue would begin in New York.

Chapter 8: Graduation Ceremony – June 2005

235 seniors marched onto the field in the scorching heat, the guys in black gowns, and the girls in red. They passed beneath an arch of black and red balloons, which were the school colors, while Pomp and Circumstance began blaring across the field. The stadium was crowded with hundreds of family members, friends and teachers. I strained to catch a glimpse of Brian and Pete in their caps and gowns, but I could hardly see anything against the full glare of the morning sun. Finally, I gave up and sank into my seat.

Principal Morley welcomed everyone to the event, followed by mousy Julie Clayton, the class valedictorian. Both Brian and Pete had hoped to earn the valedictorian spot, but the competition had been intense - sometimes fiercely so. In the end, Julie had nailed the top honor, beating them by a fraction of a point in grade point average and by having the greatest number of advanced placement and honor classes. The thing I was most struck by, however, was how bad she was at public speaking.

She had a dull-flat voice and her speech sounded scripted like she was reading from a manuscript. I wish Brian or Pete had been chosen, because at least they would have entertained the crowd. Her speech was boring and cliché, certainly nothing like the high-energy speech that Matt had delivered three years earlier when he was class valedictorian. When he took the stage, he was explosive, and you could feel the energy in the stadium drastically shift. Brimming with charisma, his speech, full of hope and joy, had pumped up the crowd. It was exhilarating to watch him take command of the stage and how people reacted to his raw energy. I wasn't sure if it was his confidence or ego, but Matt demanded attention and people gave it willingly.

I briefly looked over at Matt and wondered what he was thinking. Things had been weird between us since the night of the drunken kiss, and we had subtly avoided each other ever since. I wanted to fix the awkwardness that had settled between us, but I didn't know how to. My stomach twisted unpleasantly just thinking about it.

The next hour and 22 minutes dragged. I was uncomfortable sitting on the bleachers in the sticky June heat listening to one cripplingly boring speech after another. A massive dude in front of me obstructed my view of the stage. Every time I shifted to get a better view of the stage, so did the dude. Adding to my irritation was Matt's strange behavior. Not once did he look over at me.

I began to fidget.

Finally, despite the heat and seemingly endless supply of dull speeches, my mood improved when the students were announced, one by one, diplomas were distributed. I heard Brian's name announced, and Heather and I, along with Matt and our parents clambered to our feet just in time to catch a glimpse of him collecting his diploma.

"This is so tedious, and we are only through the C's," Heather groaned into my ear as we settled back into our seats.

"I know, I know."

Fifteen minutes later, we were finally at the N's when I saw Peter walk onto the stage. I shot to my feet and cheered at the top of my lungs when he too collected his diploma.

The ceremony finally concluded twenty minutes later with the new graduates throwing their caps into the air after graduation. Heather was behind me, followed by Matt and our parents as we made our way from the bleachers to a grassy area so that we could take family photos. We stood around griping about the blistering heat, while we waited for Brian and Pete to join us.

"Could you imagine having to wear a cap and gown in this heat?" Heather complained. I hope "it is not like this next year when we graduate."

"Tell me about it," I agreed fanning myself with my hand as I watched some random chick eyeing Matt and make her way over to him.

Heather continued to grumble about the heat, but my thoughts were on Matt and the chick. *Who was she?* Unaware of my stupid jealous emotions that were running roughshod over me, Heather continued to talk about the weather. When she got bored with that topic, she started to point out different faces in the crowd and filled me in on the local gossip: who liked whom, who was seeing whom, who was fucking whom, and who had dumped whom. For the next ten minutes I half listened to her, plastering a polite grin of interest on my face, all the while fretting over Matt. I was trying really hard not to look at him, or her, but every so often I allowed my gaze to wander back toward them and each time my irritation grew. The chick was rubbing up against him and he just stood there talking to her like it was no big deal. It was distracting and mildly repulsive.

"Hey," Heather snapped her fingers in my face twice and pointed at me with a stern expression. "Stop it."

"What?" I asked defensively.

"You know what."

"No, I don't."

"What's going on between you and Matt?"

"Nothing."

Fortunately, then, the chick walked away. With barely suppressed relief, I found myself fighting the urge to smile, returning my full attention to Heather. "What were you saying?"

"You don't fool me, Sam. You've been staring at Matt this whole time."

I rolled my eyes at her. "I have no idea what you're talking about."

"Yeah, right." Heather said, turning toward where our parents stood "Well, I'm going to go hang out with the grown-ups. Have fun ogling my brother!"

I wanted to reply to Heather with a snarky comment, but the impulse was broken when a new girl approached Matt capturing my attention once again. The new girl, a blonde amazon with huge tits, looked vaguely familiar, but I couldn't quite place her. Then I heard her annoying laugh as she giggled in his ear and it hit me like a ton of bricks, her name was Susan, and they'd gone to junior prom together. I'd always despised the girl, partly out of jealousy because she had dated Matt during high school, but also because she was a dimwitted, superficial twit who just happened to look like a swimsuit model. I tried not to look at them but snuck an accidental peek, just in time to see her put her lips to his ear and run her hand suggestively down his arm. I shuddered as she leaned in and flirted with him, poking her tongue out evocatively. It was *nasty* to witness so I frowned and gave him a sharp look of disapproval.

Matt caught me staring and our eyes met. He shrugged casually, giving me that innocent, puppy dog look that screamed, I'm the victim here and do not judge me after all the crap you've pulled. Something in his expression and how he stiffly held his body made me think back about the evening at the Boat Shack and the conversation in the Corts' kitchen the next day. "Oh, come on Matt, why are you torturing me? Do we really have to discuss Tanner and what happened?" I asked rubbing my temples.

"Harrington is bad news and I want you to promise me to stay away from him. Do you understand, Sam?" he said with a warning clear in his voice.

Our eyes met, and I swore I saw a challenge there. I thought he was being over-protective, a bit caveman *meets* big brother, but I knew that Matt had my back, and that he was truly worried about me being around Tanner. "I promise Matt to stay away from him."

"Good."

Just then, I felt a strong masculine hand on my back, and I looked up to see Brian smiling appreciatively at me. I shook my head slightly, trying to clear it from thoughts of Tanner, Matt, and that night. I smiled and yelled, "Congratulations, Brian!" and he took me in his arms and twirled me around. He removed his cap and gown, his hair sexy and disheveled looking, like he just got out of bed, so I ran my hand instinctively through it to smooth it out. Brian was pleased by the gesture, looking flushed and happy.

"Are you excited for the graduation party, Sam?" he whispered in my ear, holding me close.

"Not so fast buddy, it's photo time!" I warned playfully, pointing toward where Heather stood with our parents holding their *big-assed* digital SLR cameras as they waited for all of us under the shade of a large maple tree.

Brian wrinkled his nose in disgust. "Alright Slim, let's get this over with," he said, possessively putting his arm around me and gently guiding us over to where our parents were waiting. He started to draw invisible circles on my shoulder with his finger, making me giggle and I tickled him back. "Hey dad, take some photos of Sam and me," Brian requested, putting his arm around my waist as we posed for photographs.

I glanced behind me to see if Pete had arrived yet and that's when I noticed Matt. He was standing alone staring at us. I watched with astonishment as a slight frown formed on his face at the sight of Brian with our arms still wrapped around each other. I watched, biting my lip as his eyes narrowed and his jaw tightened. *Could he be jealous?* Matt caught me staring, and whatever emotion I thought I had seen, was quickly hidden and replaced by his perfect smile. *Had I imagined it?* Matt walked over to us then, stepping smoothly between Brian and me, clapping his brother on the back. "I'm proud of you, man!" he praised. There was no hint of jealousy in his tone, and as they laughed together, posing for the camera, I finally accepted that I was imagining something that didn't exist. Matt did not have feelings for me.

Pete came over then and I hollered "Congratulations!" wrapping him in a hug. We posed for several brother and sister photos, followed by family ones, and finally a bunch of juvenile poses. Heather and I rubbed our bodies together suggestively for a lot of silly pictures, and I thought the guys were going to combust. We started to laugh when we saw their startled expressions. Then Matt came over to me, shooting me a daring look. "May I?" he asked, wrapping his arms around me in an intimate embrace as we posed for the camera. I leaned into him and then he put his head against mine. "Comfy?" Matt whispered in my ear.

I smiled adoringly at him and moved in a little closer. "I'm perfect."

Chapter 9: Back in the Big Apple – May 2013

I stood at the baggage carousel at JFK Airport going through a mental checklist of all the things that I needed to do now that I had arrived in New York. I was so deep in thought that I didn't hear my brother approach. He came up behind me and covered my eyes with his hands, yelling, "Guess who?"

I was so startled that I practically jumped out of my skin. "Peter, are you trying to give me a heart attack or make me pee my pants?" I asked sarcastically, before punching him in the shoulder.

Peter grinned. "I've missed you, sis."

"I've missed you too." I told him genuinely. Peter and I were close, but except for a short visit during Christmas, when Peter came to London, we had not lived in the same city for almost a year. I took the time to study him carefully and admired once again how my brother had grown into such a tall, dark and handsome man. "Can't wait to see the new digs, Mr. Hotshot!"

"You'll love it. It sure pays to *bang* a real estate agent," he smirked.

"Is that so? I wouldn't know, but I'll take your word for it. Hopefully, my presence in your home, won't mess up your love life too much?"

"It's alright and the real estate agent is history, so it's good timing for a house guest. Plus, I hear we have a lot of catching up to do!" he laughed, looking very amused.

Raising an eyebrow, I glared at him with my best haughty expression. "What did mom tell you?"

"I know it *all*, babe," he remarked, a silly grin on his face. "Wish I could have been a fly on the wall for the happy reunion."

I gritted my teeth, refusing to acknowledge his remarks. After that, we busied ourselves with getting my luggage from the carousel.

"So how was it seeing them after so much time?" he asked, his amused expression, now turning serious.

I shrugged my shoulders while deliberating my answer. "It was surreal," I finally said, chewing my lip.

"And?" he prompted.

"And nice. I've missed having them in my life."

"All of them?" he asked, the skepticism clear on his face.

"Yes Pete, I've missed all of them and if it's possible, I hope to have a relationship with each and every one of them."

"What type of relationship?" he prompted. "After all, I wouldn't want to dirty up my brand-new suits by having to beat up Brian or Matt again."

"Is that supposed to make me laugh Peter?" I grumbled. "Stick to your day job, because comedy is definitely NOT in your future."

"Touchy, Sam. I see you left your humor back in London."

With the amount of luggage, I had, the topic of the Cort family was quickly dropped. Peter had rented a limo, which was a nice surprise. During the ride through the city, and back to his place, Peter filled me in on his work at Blackstone, where he was a Senior Managing Director in the Investor Relations & Business Development Group. We talked about my upcoming interview there and with whom I would meet. In addition to Blackstone, I also had interviews scheduled with Warburg Pincus, Goldman Sachs, and some of the smaller investment banking boutique firms. I very much wanted to discuss with Peter the job offer with the Cort Group, but decided that I would hold off until we were comfortably settled back at his place.

***

"Wow, this place is amazing. I guess you really are a big shot now!" I commented with pleasure, as I walked around admiring his bright and airy two-bedrooms two-bath condo, located in the financial district. "Can you walk to work from here?"

"I sure can," he smiled proudly. "It takes about fifteen minutes."

"Nice!" I complimented, and then excused myself to unpack in the guest room, which was spacious by New York standards. After unpacking, I took a shower in the über luxurious marble guest bathroom that had one of those decadent spa-like shower systems. You know the kind that featured so many bells and whistles that it was basically a hedonistic paradise.

"This is really nice. I'm proud of you," I said to Peter as I walked into the living room and jumped on the comfy couch. "By the way, that shower was better than the one in the master bathroom at the Corts' house. I may never leave."

"Is that so," he chuckled coming over to the couch with wine and snacks for us to nibble on. "Is that a threat?"

"Ha! You are so *not* funny, Peter."

"Yes, you've pointed that out already, sister dear."

We bantered like this back and forth, and it was comfortable and familiar. I loved London, and being close to my mom and dad, but somehow hanging out with my brother and being in New York felt more real. Although it wasn't where we grew up in New England, it was close enough, and I finally felt like I had returned home after a very long absence.

Peter and I caught up on each other's lives and talked about everything, but the one subject that was at the forefront of my thoughts. It remained the elephant in the room for hours and I wondered how to bring it up, but I didn't have to worry, because Peter breached the subject first. "When are we going to talk about it?"

I looked him squarely in the eye. "What do you want to know?"

"Whatever you want to tell me."

I told him about running into Mr. Cort at the Private Equity Summit, and how it felt to see Matt, Brian and Heather again after so much time. I stopped my story once to tell Peter that I had given Brian his phone number and that Brian planned to contact him. Then, I told him about the job offer and where I had left things during the dinner with the Cort family. Finally, I concluded that I was confused by the experience and scared by my conflicting emotions, because I was both relieved and panicked by the prospect of having them back in my life.

"That certainly is a lot to take in." Peter said, getting up from the couch and stretching his legs. He put his chin in his hand and gazed out the window. He looked pensive, and deep in thought.

"Clearly." I said, joining him by the window, and rustling his hair. "Do you think I'm crazy to consider the job offer?"

"In an insane world, nothing is crazy," he said sardonically.

I busted out laughing and made a circular motion with my index finger at my ear to indicate that I thought my brother was crazy. "What does that mean, Peter?"

"I don't know, but it sounded good," he offered, and laughed. Then he stared down at me and shrugged his shoulders in what appeared to be an ironic gesture. "Do you ever wonder what would have happened if you hadn't shut them out in the first place?"

"Every day," I said wistfully, with a laugh that tried to hide my regret.

"Don't be sad, Sam. You can't erase the past."

"I know that," I mumbled distractedly, as memories from long ago invaded my thoughts.

"Why do you want to take the job?" Peter suddenly asked. "Don't get me wrong, it's a great opportunity and Tom Cort and his sons, especially Matt, are brilliant. Probably among the most brilliant men I have ever known. Matt essentially is willing to work his ass off and that's why the New York office has had such tremendous growth and success in a few short years. You would certainly learn a lot if you work with them, but what are your motives for doing so?"

I anxiously rubbed my hands together and started flitting around the apartment as I tried to explain my reasoning to my brother. "Well, you've summed up a lot of why it would be appealing for me to work with them. I have always admired how the Corts simply pursue their vision of excellence in whatever they do, and as for Matt, I've always been bowled over by how his brain works a little bit faster than anybody else's. A girl could certainly learn a lot from a brain like that."

"Do you realize that Matt's quick-wittedness almost drove Brian to the breaking point?" Peter said arching an eyebrow at me. "It's not always easy being around someone so naturally-gifted and perfect. It would make a lesser man or woman crumble."

"First, Matt is far from perfect which you and I know from personal experience. Second, are you calling me a lesser woman, Pete? If so, I'll kick your ass!"

He chuckled and raised his hands in a gesture of mock surrender. "I didn't mean it as an insult, Sam, just a warning. I'll never forget how frustrated Brian got every time he thought he did something perfectly, only to find out Matt had done it better. The difference was marginal, I mean like 3.95 to 3.97, but to Brian it would be the end of the world, and he would be so deflated."

"Are you forgetting how well I know them?" I asked sarcastically. "I'm well aware of Brian's jealousy and Matt's holier-than-thou attitude!"

"So, if you took the job it would be for professional reasons only?" he asked tilting his head in my direction and giving me what I took to be a rather pointed look.

"Well," I paused to consider his question, while still trying to organize my conflicting thoughts on the subject. "For the most part, it would be for professional reasons, but I won't deny that I've had a huge gaping hole in my life without Heather, Matt, and Brian in my life. I've missed them and if I accepted the job, it would allow me a lot of time and interaction with at least Matt and Brian again. That's tempting and hard to turn down."

He pulled back, arching an eyebrow. "You could rebuild a relationship with them without having to accept the job."

I swallowed and nodded, looking at him. "Of course, I could, but by seeing them on a daily basis, it speeds up the process," I admitted sheepishly.

His eyes met mine slowly, a serious expression on his face. "I just have to say it, Sam," he replied, his tone humorless.

I met his eyes. "What?"

"When you say rebuild relations, do you mean with them or do you mean with him?" he asked holding my gaze. His tone was quiet, and unnaturally subdued, but I couldn't help but feel that he was accusing me.

I shrugged my shoulders casually and glanced through the oversized windows that flanked the northern and eastern walls of Peter's 9th floor corner apartment, illuminating the room with a nice glow from the setting sun.

"What would you say if I told you that both the Cort brothers were married?" Peter suddenly asked.

"What?" I shrieked. I could feel my heart rate increase. "Are they married?"

"I highly doubt it Sam, but I wanted to test your reaction, and you failed miserably," Peter said, laughing quietly and shaking his head.

My cheeks flushed and I was embarrassed by my response and that Peter had caught me. I finally turned to him, trying to bluff my way out of it. "I was just surprised, that's all Peter," I lied. "I think Matt and Brian are a little young for marriage. Besides, I didn't see any rings."

"Oh, they're not that young, Sam. I thought Matt was approaching 30."

"Not until January." I blurted out while Peter stared at me with an amused grin on his face. "Oh my god, Pete, so I remember his birthday. It's no big deal."

Peter was grinning now, and it was a massive grin, that showed off his perfect pearly white teeth. "Objectively speaking, you're right. It's nothing, nothing at all." He laughed and winked at me, as he pulled me toward the doorway, effectively ending the conversation. "Come on, Sam, I'm starving. Let's go out to dinner."

As I followed my brother out the door, I groaned internally and chastised myself for saying too much. My brother could always read me, and I had unwittingly shown him too much of my hand. If I was this obvious around Peter, how could I possibly keep my scattered emotions in check around the Corts, especially around him? *I was royally screwed.*

After all this time, and everything that happened, I had never forgotten him. I had tried desperately to get him out of my head, but once the hurt and anger subsided, all that was left were memories of all the good times and loving moments we shared. No matter how many boyfriends or relationships I had, he was always swimming around in the back of my head, popping up at the most inconvenient times. I loathed admitting it, but I had never found a replacement guy to win my heart. Over the years, when I met someone new, I had an obnoxious habit of comparing the new guy to the Cort brothers. I know, I know – bad Sammy. Even with all the crap that happened, the Cort brothers epitomized in my head – the perfect men. Believe me, I knew they were hardly perfect, but I still had a tough time discarding my schoolgirl fantasy. *Like I said, I was royally fucked.*

Chapter 10: Graduation Party – June 2005

Brian and Peter's graduation party was like no other with a photo booth, inflatable bouncy house, and even a mechanical bull! And though it was 90 plus degrees outside with a humidity level of 80%, nothing could ruin the celebration. The party was held in the Corts' backyard. Because alcohol was served, my dad and Mr. Cort were stationed at the party's entrance and collected keys from every teen that showed. The Corts had rented a shuttle service to bring guests home or they could choose to stay and leave the next morning.

Once guests passed the entrance, they were greeted with a hand painted welcome sign that said, "Welcome to Brian & Pete's Awesome Graduation Party! Please grab a hat and glow stick!" Next to the sign, were two giant galvanized buckets, one filled with funny party hats and the other filled with white glow sticks to help people navigate the semi-darkened grounds.

Single strands of twinkling lights hung from backyard trees, and festive lanterns lined the tables, walkways, swimming pool, and stairs that led directly below to the dock and boat house, creating a dreamy glow that made the yard look like a fairyland.

An army of "grill-masters" sizzled steak tips, slow-cooked baby back ribs, spicy BBQ shrimp, hamburgers, and hot dogs on massive grills that lined the patio. There was even a rotisserie chicken!

I was watching the sunset over the water with Heather and Ryan, when Brian and a couple of his buddies came over. They reeked of marijuana. "Are you baked?" I asked.

Brian grinned widely at me and shrugged. "Nah."

"Oh my god. You are!"

"Am not!" Brian cracked up. "How about a game of chicken?"

I leaned in and shook my head no.

He grinned. "Oh yeah, you are so getting wet!" Before I could protest further, he picked me up princess style and carried me over to the swimming pool.

"Brian, if you dunk me into the pool while I'm still fully dressed, I will kill you!"

Brian chuckled. He was really, really baked, but he listened to me and gingerly placed me down by the edge of the pool. "Fine Slim. Go change into a swimsuit."

"Come on!" Heather called. "You can borrow one from me."

I followed her into the house and up to her bedroom. "Are you kidding me?" I squealed, as she handed me what looked like two tiny triangles of fabric attached to a string. The bikini left very little up to the imagination. In fact, it was so small it practically could fit into a pillbox.

Heather smiled innocently and shrugged her shoulders. "What's the problem?" she asked in an overly sweet voice. "You have a nice body so flaunt it. That's my motto and that's the only extra bikini I have, so suck it up, Sam! I'll be down at the pool waiting," she said huffily slamming the door behind her.

Ten minutes later, I put on the offending piece of material and stared at my reflection in the mirror. The string bikini was obscene, and I was mortified to wear it in public. I glanced backwards at the mirror one last time, and then I straightened my shoulders and walked down the stairs. When I reached the bottom step, I practically walked right into Matt, whom I hadn't seen since the graduation ceremony earlier that day. When he saw me, his eyes appraised me up and down. Goose bumps spread across my skin and I shivered slightly, as he moved closer, staring intently at me. "Nice bikini."

"Um, thanks. It's Heather's doing."

"She has good taste," he murmured taking a step forward.

I winced. "You think?"

"Yeah I do."

I laughed nervously as I watched him close the gap between us. His gaze never left mine and I suddenly felt jumpy and anxious. He stopped and stood in front of me. "Nervous Sam?" he said, leaning towards me, almost like he wanted to kiss me.

Oh, was I nervous! But I held his gaze and answered smoothly. "What do you mean?"

He took a step closer and ran his fingers through my hair, his grin widening, and then he whispered in my ear. "When I left for college you were a kid. What happened?"

"I don't know," I mumbled, biting down on my lip to suppress a nervous sigh from escaping. Matt's proximity was wreaking havoc on my emotions.

Just then, Brian came in. "There you are, Sam! I've been waiting for you." He sauntered over, standing between Matt and me. "Hey bro," he said, "you mind if I steal her away?"

"Brian." Matt acknowledged, slipping his fingers away from my hair and taking a step away from me. "What are you up to?"

"Sam is going to be my partner in a little friendly competition of Chicken!"

"Yes, but…"

"No but, Sam," Brian interrupted.

"K." I replied. "Did you want to join us, Matt?"

"No, thanks," Matt replied lightly. "You guys have fun. I should probably say hello to some of the guests."

I was disappointed that Matt wasn't going to join us, and was confused by his mixed signals, but I could do nothing but nod and say goodbye.

"Alright bro, we'll catch up with you later." Then Brian surprised me and lifted me off the ground. "You're all mine" he joked, carrying me outside and throwing me in the pool. He quickly followed with a cannonball jump, splashing everyone in the pool. Soon after, we split into teams of two for a chicken fight, which was basically a game of "shoulder wars" where one person sat on her teammate's shoulders, wrestling the other team until someone fell over. Brian picked me, putting me on his shoulders. There were five other teams, including my brother Peter, who mounted Heather on his shoulders. The highlight of the game was when I knocked Heather down, and Brian and I laughed non-stop as she shrieked at us.

I had so much fun in the water, that I forgot my earlier modesty over the string bikini and let myself cut loose and enjoy the party without reservation. An hour later, fireworks painted the sky over the water, and I marveled not only at the spectacle, but how much the Corts must have paid for Brian and Pete's graduation party. I decided to get out of the pool so that I could watch the fireworks from a better spot. I heard Matt's voice the moment I stepped out of the pool. "Stay there, I'll get you a towel." A tiny shiver went through me when he came into view. Matt wrapped a towel around me and started to rub my arms for warmth. We never exchanged a word, but something passed between us and I knew in that instinct, that I wasn't imagining it. Matt was drawn to me too.

A second later, Brian was out of the pool standing behind me, and Matt released me pulling away. "Hey bro, let me get you a towel," Matt said, swiping a towel from a pile in the corner and throwing it hard at Brian.

Brian grabbed it and chuckled. "Is that the best you can do?" he said hurling the towel back at Matt. Matt laughed and tossed another towel at Brian, this time with great force, smacking Brian in the head. They started wrestling, and I couldn't decide if they were behaving like little boys or total jackasses. I shook my head, pulled my sundress over my damp bikini, and walked away to view the fireworks. A few minutes later, Brian and Matt joined me, and we watched the fireworks in companionable silence.

When the fireworks ended, Brian leaned into me and whispered in my ear, "Can I talk to you privately for a minute?" I nodded my consent, slightly puzzled by his request. He turned to Matt, who was watching us intently, his brow furrowed. "We will be back soon."

Matt closed his eyes momentarily, and then he gave Brian a curt nod, before turning, and walking away from us. Brian offered me his hand and we walked across the sloping grass toward the clump of trees at the farthest edge of the lawn. The same secluded spot where I had first met Matt and Brian a decade earlier.

When we came to a complete stop, Brian took both my hands in his, his expression turning serious as he waited for me to look at him. I stared at Brian expectantly. "What's up?" I asked, the concern clear in my voice.

For a moment, he looked lost and hesitant. "I'm not sure how to begin." he said quietly, almost like he was speaking to himself. "You know I like you, right?"

Stepping away from his adoring gaze, I looked down at my feet and bit my lip, not sure how to respond. He put his finger beneath my chin, forcing me to look at him as he waited for me to say something. "Yes," I finally responded.

"I want us to go out," he stated, almost defiantly, "On a date. What do you think?"

"U-um," I struggled to find the right words. *I had no idea what to say.* I wiped my sweaty hands on my sundress and played nervously with a loose thread that was hanging from my skirt. "Brian, it makes no sense. You leave this coming week for the summer and then you'll be off to college."

"I'll be back for a few weeks in August and then Brown is only 90-minutes away. We could make it work Sam. Let's give it a try?"

"I'm not sure," I blurted out, feeling a little panicky. "We've known each other our whole lives Brian, and I don't want to spoil our friendship."

He looked momentarily dismayed by my answer, but then he cocked his head adorably and winked at me. "Promise me that you'll at least think about it?" he demanded; his blue eyes bright with feeling. "Okay?"

I looked up to meet his expectant gaze and took a deep breath before speaking. "Okay. I'll think about its Brian."

Believing that our conversation was finished, I turned toward the direction of the party, desperately wanting to flee. My mind was reeling with thousands of questions racing around my head, each of them leading back to Matt. My thoughts were interrupted when Brian gripped my hand, a vulnerable, adorable expression on his face. "Just one more thing, Sam." He said sounding worried, as he fidgets with the towel around his neck.

"Try not to fall in love with anyone while I'm gone this summer."

I squeezed his hand and gave him a reassuring smile as we made our way back to the party.

Chapter 11: A Change of Plans – June 2013

The Cort Group's New York office was in the GM Building, a 50-story marble-clad office tower on Fifth Avenue overlooking Central Park and was a few blocks away from Bloomingdale's. As I quickly passed by the department store's window display, a pair of Stuart Weitzman strappy open-toed heels caught my eye, and I knew that they would pair well with my new linen Capri pants to make a perfect work-to-weekend outfit. Of course, that was assuming I got a job soon. With that realization, I looked at my watch and sped up my pace, as I didn't want to be late. I was still slightly annoyed at the last-minute rescheduled meeting time. Originally, I was slated to meet with Mr. Cort, Matt, and Brian the next morning at 11:00 a.m. followed by lunch, but those plans had changed. Instead, I received a call this morning from an Anna Chen, who identified herself as Matthew Cort's executive assistant, apologizing on his behalf and asking if I could come to the Cort Group that evening at 5:00 p.m. to meet with Matthew Cort as he was flying to D.C. the next morning. I wanted to say no, because the thought of meeting with Matt alone scared the shit out of me, but I knew that I had to get it over with sooner or later, especially if I wanted to work there.

As I jostled among the throngs of people on the very crowded New York City sidewalks, I began to mentally prepare myself for what lay ahead. After reading several articles on the top advisory and asset management firms; it was clear that the Cort Group was known for showing it had *big boy chops* and was experiencing rapid growth, while still maintaining a stellar reputation. The Cort Group had a reputation for only hiring "all-stars" and the recruiting process was known to be rigorous. I realized that it was only due to my close personal relationship with the family that I had been offered a job without having to go through this meticulous process.

Before entering the office tower, I filled my lungs with one last breath of the warm June air, and it occurred to me, albeit fleetingly, that it was almost eight years ago today that I had gone sailing with Matt and agreed to be a member of his 9-person crew for the Berringer Bowl, an overnight race from

Marblehead to Provincetown. I pushed the thought away as quickly as it appeared. To say that I was unnerved would be an understatement.

I shook my head and cursed as I entered the GM Building lobby. After receiving a visitor's pass from the security desk, I walked over to the bank of elevators, and pushed the button for the 26th floor. When I got off the elevator, I quickly looked at my reflection in the lobby mirror. I was wearing my favorite baby blue blouse with a patterned blue and white form-fitting pencil skirt that I had bought in London with my mother. The first time I tried it on, my mother gushed and said, "Samantha, you cut a stunning figure in that skirt and it really shows off your super slender figure." I teamed it with white high heels and wore my dark hair back in a bun. Finally, I completed the look with a black and nickel French luxury leather briefcase that had been a graduation present from my parents. Straightening my shoulders, I looked one last time at the reflection in the mirror, and I knew that I projected the image of a young, beautiful and confident woman. *It was show time!*

The moment you walked into the offices of the Cort Group, you were greeted with hustle and bustle, and stunning views of Central Park and the New York City skyline. The office radiated a sense of excitement, and it was filled with a lot of energy and movement, much like the personality of the founding family. The interior was fresh, modern, and open, but dignified at the same time with a mixture of dark wood and glass. As I waited at the reception area, I chuckled to myself as my eyes followed a staircase up to a second level where I saw three glass-walled meeting rooms with the mathematical symbol for Pi painted on each exterior glass wall, respectively 1π, 2π, 3π.

A smartly dressed Indian woman greeted me and asked if I would care for something to drink. After refusing, I followed her through a wide-open corridor with subtle, elegant lighting, and a subdued color scheme that led to several glass-walled offices, and a second, smaller waiting area filled with natural light from a glass wall facing the park. Completing the space were brown leather couches, wood furnishings, a fish tank, and a flat screen television.

The Indian woman addressed a small attractive Asian woman who was wearing rather severe looking square glasses. The Asian woman shook my hand and introduced herself. "Hello, Samantha, I'm Anna Chen, Matthew Cort's assistant."

"It's a pleasure to meet you Anna."

"I'm sorry, but Mr. Cort is running late from another meeting. He apologized and asked if you could wait. Please be seated," she said indicating her hand toward a plush leather couch. "Mr. Cort should be here shortly.

She gave a slight nod of acknowledgement and then I heard her high heels on the wood floor as she walked away. I put my briefcase down and went over to the glass wall overlooking Central Park. The view was spectacular and later I thought it would be nice to kick off my fancy shoes and walk barefoot through the freshly cutgrass. I loved this time of year; the transition from spring to summer. It was my favorite time, because the weather was warming up, the flowers were blooming, and everything seemed light, hopeful, and full of possibility.

I continued to look out the window, lost in thought, for quite some time. I didn't hear him enter the room, until he cleared his throat to speak. "Sam, I'm so sorry that I kept you waiting, but it's been one hell of a day."

I turned away from the window, and my heart quickened as I looked up into his handsome face as he approached me. His usual, perfectly smooth hair was an unruly mess, his suit jacket gone with his shirt unbuttoned, his tie loosened, and the sleeves of his blue dress shirt rolled up past his elbows.

"No worries. You look tired; do you want to reschedule?"

"No," he said, "but let's get out of here and talk outside in the courtyard or in the park. Follow me while I collect a few papers in my office and then we can go."

I bent down to retrieve my briefcase and followed him into his glass-walled office, which shared the same amazing view as the one that I had just admired from the waiting area. As he stuffed papers into his briefcase, my eyes perused his office and landed on a small-scale version of the Cortship sailboat that was displayed on his desk. My cheeks flushed red as memories of our time on the boat came flooding back, and I turned away from him, acutely aware that he was watching me intently.

"Ready Sam?" he asked standing behind me and ushering us toward the doorway. We were interrupted numerous times by various people that had to talk with him for 'a quick sec' (which turned out to be a heck of a longtime) and then finally Matt escorted me back through the lobby to the bank of elevators.

He smiled at me as we rode the elevator down together in silence. "Courtyard or park?" he finally asked when we were down in the lobby.

"Most definitely, the park, but don't judge me too harshly when I remove my shoes," I smirked.

"Park it is!" he said with a flourish. "Now the really important question, bench or grass?"

"Grass, please," I requested with enthusiasm.

Always the perfect gentleman, Matt opened doors, offered me his hand when navigating steps and cobblestones, and when we arrived inside the park, he placed his jacket on a nice spot of grass and told me to sit on it so that I wouldn't ruin my outfit. I did as he asked and waited expectantly for him to talk while I removed my shoes and breathed in the lovely warm air. He put his hand in his hair and our eyes met and lingered while I waited for him to talk. There was no way that I was going to speak first.

"Thanks, Sam, for meeting with me so late and for the venue change. I'll cover a couple of broad strokes about the firm tonight and tomorrow you'll get a formal tour of the office when you meet with my dad and Brian and they should be able to answer any questions you might have."

"Sounds good, Matt," I answered smoothly; my tone was crisp and business-like.

"But before we get to that…"

He paused, his eyes searching my face, and cleared his throat.

Oh no, here it comes. I braced myself for him to continue.

"We need to talk about our relationship and how we move forward from here, whether in a business or personal context," he said, his eyes fixed on me. "It's imperative that you stop running from the past and that you finally tell me how you feel, and I'll do the same."

I was stunned into silence by his candor and straightforward manner. I knew that the conversation was coming, and that we had to talk, but I forgot just how assertive and direct he could be. "Ok," I stammered quietly not meeting his gaze.

Bending at the knees, Matt crouched down next to me and grasped my hand, bringing him level with my eyes. "I'm sorry for hurting you, Sam," he said sincerely, his voice thick with emotion. "Obviously, I handled things poorly that summer and I should have been honest with you from the very start. I was wrong. I hope you can find it in your heart to forgive me?"

"It was a long time ago Matt, so don't beat yourself up about it. It's ancient history and I'm fine," I lied, pulling my hands away from him.

"Are you fine?" he questioned; his gaze unwavering.

I absentmindedly twirled a strand of hair that had fallen out of my bun around my finger. "Uh-huh," I answered lowering my gaze from him and causing my hand to shake slightly.

"I don't believe you."

"Do we really have to revisit the past?" I questioned softly. "Isn't it enough to let bygones be bygones?"

"If you want to be my friend or business associate, you need to learn to trust me Sam, and I need to know that when the going gets tough you won't run away again."

"You're practically a genius, Matt. Of course, I trust your business acumen and I know I will learn a lot if I join the firm. Professionally, you can always count on me."

"Do you think I'm trustworthy?" he asked, his voice soft, and imploring.

I met his eyes and shrugged my shoulders.

"Why do you do that?" he asked.

"Do what?" I asked innocently.

"You deflect the question and never really answer anything."

"That's not true."

He leaned closer to me and raised his eyebrow. "Come on, Sam. We both know it *is* true."

"Fine," I said, a slight tremor in my voice. "What do you want to know? I'll answer *any* question?"

"Will you ever be able to completely trust me again?" His voice was strained, needy.

I hesitated. He had captured the crux of the problem with his question. *Could I trust him again?* "I don't know," I murmured not meeting his gaze.

Sitting back, I could feel him watching me. His voice was low. "Why did you run?" he said softly.

I stared at him for a moment and then looked over his shoulder at two boys playing Frisbee in the distance. "You broke my heart," I stated simply.

"I know and I'm sorry," he said gently, pulling my chin up with his index finger. "It was my fault, but you ran away and never gave me a chance to fix it. Do you know how that felt for me for you to avoid me so completely and to ignore all my emails, phone calls and attempts to see you? It was torture, and not only did I lose you, but it strained my relationship with my family for years."

"I never meant to come between you and your family."

"I know that Sam," he said getting up from his crouching position and running his hand through his hair. "I know what happened between us hurt other people and I'm sorry about that. But at the same time, I don't regret what happened between us that summer. My only regret is how I handled things, and the position I put you in. But you should know that my feelings for you were genuine, and that I never forgot you."

I stood up warily, unsure of what I wanted to say. I walked over to him, and gently reached out to place my hand on his elbow. "Thank you for saying that Matt. It means a lot.

"Thank you," he said, his hands suddenly wrapping around my waist, pulling me into a hug. The embrace felt comforting and familiar, and I laughed despite my inner turmoil, resting my hands against his chest and burying my face in his neck. His touch felt good. It felt like home.

Chapter 12: The 'Cortship' begins – June 2005

My skin was flushed, whether from the sun, the unrelenting June heat, or because of the proximity of Matthew Cort, I wasn't sure. We were sailing on the Corts' IMX 40 Danish race-ready yacht, the Cortship. From Marblehead to Gloucester harbor, and the boat was fast. I'm talking grand-prix fast! It was a lean, mean racing machine and as we picked up speed, we left what looked like an almost perfect V shaped aquatic trail, like a flock of geese heading south, across the calm waters of the Atlantic Ocean.

"Sam, could you throw me the sun block?" Matt yelled over the sound of the wind and crashing waves.

I reluctantly turned away from the spray of the wild, open water and went searching through our bag of supplies for the sun block. "I can do one better, I can hand it to you," I teased coming over to him and giving him the sun block.

"Thanks, smart ass!" he grinned taking the sun block from me. Then unexpectedly he took his shirt off. "Could you apply some cream to my shoulders and back?"

The image of him shirtless made me momentarily speechless and I froze in my tracks as my eyes lingered on his hard stomach and rippling muscles. "Um." I mumbled. "What did you say?"

He gave me a knowing, self-righteous smile at catching me staring at him. "See something you like, Sam?"

I raised my eyes to him and quickly erased the guilty expression on my face. Believe me, Tanner Harrington was *not* the only conceited, arrogant guy around town. "I think you're delusional Matt. Obviously, you're in need of hydration!" I said quickly, walking over to the supplies and grabbing a bottle of water.

"If you say so," he smirked, taking the water from me and handing me the lotion. "Could you please apply the sun block now?"

I squeezed the lotion into my hands and tentatively massaged it over his back, shoulders and forearms. Feeling the familiar pull between us, my hand lingered along his lower spine, before reluctantly pulling away. "All set," I mumbled, before turning and walking away.

I was drawn to him in a way I'd never known. During the graduation party, I was convinced that Matt had felt *it* too. But after the conversation with Brian, Matt had kept his distance from me, and I wondered if I had imagined the whole thing. Don't get me wrong, there was definitely some sort of tension between us, but I wasn't experienced enough to know *what or if* it meant anything to him? Even if Matt did feel it, perhaps it didn't mean the same thing to him as it did for me, and the many girls that came before me.

Over the years, I had seen a bevy of the prettiest, most popular girls dazzled by Matthew Cort. I would never forget the heartbreak I felt at age ten when I discovered that Matt was "dating" his first girlfriend, Becky Thompson. Of course, the eighth grade "relationship" only lasted a few weeks, but my relief over the pair's demise was short-lived when he started to "date" Julie Kendall the following week. Then, a week later, there was a replacement. After that, Matt was never single for long.

When I thought back of all the girls who had loved Matt, it became painfully obvious that he was out of my league. Matthew Cort could have *any* girl he wanted, so why would he ever choose me?

It wasn't that I was insecure. I knew that I was no longer "Slim," the plain skinny tomboy with boring brown hair. With my seventeenth birthday, I had transformed from the ugly duckling and turned into the beautiful swan. And I knew I had brains too.

But even with all that I had going for me, Matt still seemed out of reach, and that's how I came to really understand Brian Cort and what made him tick.

Brian was incredibly handsome, bright, and universally loved, but he always lagged behind his "all-star" big brother. To use an analogy, if the Cort brothers competed in the Olympics,

Brian would win a silver medal, and the gold would go to Matt. It wasn't Matt's fault that he seemed to effortlessly dominate everything he tried. But for those around him, it sometimes became difficult to deal with that level of perfection on a daily basis. Brian should not consider himself a lesser man, because he was not inferior to Matt, but Brian didn't see himself clearly, and I guess neither did I.

***

We docked the Cortship in Gloucester around lunchtime and walked around the working Harbor Cove area to a waterfront promenade. The afternoon heat was intense, but I hardly noticed, as we sat on a bench comfortably enjoying each other's company. It had been almost two years since the last time we had gone sailing together and I had missed his company and friendship. There had always been something very calming about Matt, and I felt content when we were together. I felt like he really understood me and that I could tell him things that I didn't feel comfortable sharing with others.

We walked over to a waterfront restaurant for lunch and ate outside on the deck. As we bonded over burgers and lemonade, he told me about his time at Stanford. He knew that Stanford was my first choice and he encouraged me to apply for early admission in the fall, and recommended teachers and classes that I should take *if* I went there.

After lunch, we returned to the boat and companionably worked together getting ready to launch the boat for takeoff.

"You've become a very competent sailor, Sam," Matt said, cocking his head in my direction, his dark hair falling over his forehead, somehow making him look even sexier. "I think it's time you take the next step in your sailing education and sail in the Berringer Bowl, as part of the Cortship crew. What do you say Sam, would you like to join our crew for the race?"

I was momentarily floored by his offer, and secretly pleased that he trusted me enough to even suggest joining his crew for the overnight race from Marblehead to Provincetown, Cape Cod. "I'm thrilled that you've asked me Matt, but I've never competed in a race before and I don't want to let you and the team down," I admitted shyly.

"You won't let us down," he said, unflinching. "And. I wouldn't ask you if I didn't think you were ready."

"But open-water racing is serious and can be dangerous," I pointed out.

"I know that you're ready for this challenge, Sam, and it's a short overnight leg, so it's a good primer for you to start with; he said, never wavering with his support. "I think you'll find the experience exhilarating and fulfilling. I would never put you or the crew in a dangerous position. Ideally, I like to race with a crew of 8 to 10, so you would fill back up for Bow, Mast and various other positions. It would be a great learning experience and the best part is that we can kick Tanner's ass together."

"Tanner?" I questioned. "But the Sailfish is a 38-foot Farr sailboat in the PHRF B class program and the Cortship races in the A class, so how can we compete against Tanner?"

"Apparently, the Harrington's have a new boat, the Sailfish II, that will compete in the A class. Tanner registered for the Berringer Bowl a few days after I entered the competition. Convenient, eh?" he asked, raising an eyebrow in my direction.

I met his eyes, understanding passing between us. "Let's kick his ass!" I stated with determination.

He laughed and nodded. "That's my girl!" he said, excited. "But I have to warn you, if you commit to this, the training schedule is fairly strenuous."

"How strenuous?" I asked cautiously.

"For the rest of June, and all of July, we will need to be on the water at least two to three nights per week practicing with the crew, as well as participating in every Wednesday night's race," he stated, carefully watching me for my reaction. "Starting Monday, I'll be working at the Cort Group full-time for the summer, but I can practice tacking, gibing, and the different roles on the boat with you on the weekends so that you'll be more experienced with big boat racing. How does that sound?"

I smiled broadly at him, with the realization that by doing this boat race, we would be required to spend almost all of June and July together. "Sounds good, Matt," I said trying my best to keep my voice calm and casual. Suddenly, this summer was turning into the *best summer of my life* and had only just begun.

Chapter 13: Back at the Cort Group – June 2013

As I waited at the reception desk of the Cort Group, for the second time in twenty-four hours, I chuckled again, when my eyes landed on the three glass-walled meeting rooms, respectively 1π, 2π, and 3π, and my mind wandered to the previous night when Matt walked me home.

"Who decided to name the meeting rooms in the office after the symbol for Pi?" I asked him with an absurd grin on my face.

"Whom do you think?" he answered, a hint of a smirk pulling at the corner of his lips.

"Well, I knew for sure it wasn't Brian," I joked.

"Ha! That's an understatement!" Matt agreed, shaking his head sarcastically. "Brian still gives me grief about the name, and it's been four years."

I immediately grinned. "I knew it was you!" Then I turned away and laughed softly to myself at the realization of just how well I knew him, and his brother, a fact that both frightened and comforted me. We walked quietly for a moment, and I started to move a pebble across the grass with my toe. We continued to walk through the park in companionable silence, and I was grateful that we seemed to be learning to be at ease around each other without having to make a lot of awkward small talk. It was only a simple walk, but after eight years of hurt and anger, it felt nice to enjoy his company again, something that I thought we had lost forever.

When we were back on pavement, a few blocks from Peter's condo, I started to retrieve my high heels and thank him for the walk.

"Care for a hand?" he inquired, when he noticed me struggling with my shoes.

I nodded and leaned forward, grasping his shoulder for support, while I carefully slipped on my shoes. I straightened up and was about to pull away, when suddenly, out of nowhere, his hands moved to rest on my hips, and I felt that inexplicable draw between us. And then, aware of what he had done, he quickly removed his hold on my hips, and took a step back. "I'm really sorry Sam."

I blinked to clear my head. "No harm, no foul." I said, trying to sound light and casual, and not think about how it felt to have his achingly familiar hands on me. My head was spinning from his proximity and I immediately felt overwhelmed by his presence, instinctively wanting to flee. "Hey Matt, it's only a few more blocks to Peter's, so I can walk the rest of the way myself."

"Are you sure?" "How about I hail you a cab?" He said, his tone serious and over-protective.

"I prefer to walk Matt."

"Okay, but it's going to be dark soon, so be careful, Sam, and don't stop anywhere," he said, raising his voice with authority to make sure I heard his point.

"I will Matt. Thanks for the walk and for holding my briefcase, but could I have it back now?"

"On one condition," he said, a wicked smile on his face. "Have dinner with me?"

Surprised, I stood there dumbly, not sure how to respond.

"Come on Sam, I'll be back from D.C. on Friday and you have to eat anyway, so how about it?"

"I can't Friday."

His eyes narrowed briefly. "Oh yeah … Do you have a hot date?"

"Yeah," I giggled. "With your sister."

"Oh, you're seeing Heather," he responded, sounding relieved. "That's good. I know that she has missed you."

"I missed her too."

"Well then, how about Saturday night?"

"You have Saturday night *free*?" I asked, a little skeptical.

Matt laughed. "I could *if* you say yes."

"I'm sorry, but I have plans."

His head shot up and our eyes met. "Oh, so Saturday night *is* a hot date?"

"I'm seeing an old friend from college."

"Male or female?" he asked fishing for information.

"Actually, an old boyfriend," I admitted, avoiding his eyes.

He stood facing me, his voice low. "Was it serious?"

The question hung in the air until I finally stood straighter and raised my eyes to him. "That's personal Matt and none of your business."

His eyes bore into me and for several seconds he stood there studying me, looking anxious. "Well," he uttered in a tight tone, "if you don't think Saturday will be a late night, how about an early morning run, followed by Sunday brunch?"

I knew what Matt was trying to ask in his round about manner. *Was I planning on sleeping with my ex-boyfriend on*

Saturday night? It was none of Matt's business what I did in my personal life or with whom. The unspoken dialogue between us was irritating the crap out of me and I wanted to tell him to take a leap off the George Washington Bridge, but instead I surprised myself and found myself accepting his invitation for Sunday.

"Great, I'll pick you up at your place at 6 a.m. on Sunday," he said decisively. "After we run, do you think Peter will mind if I shower there?"

"You're welcome to shower at Pete's place, but you're NUTS if you think I'm running at that ungodly hour on a Sunday morning!"

"Are you getting soft on me, Sam?" he challenged in a lighthearted manner. "Remember the early bird catches the worm."

"Not this bird," I protested stubbornly.

"Fine," he said rolling his eyes. "I'll be there at 7:00 a.m." Without waiting for an answer, he handed me back my briefcase, kissed me on the forehead lightly, and turned to leave. By the time I thought to protest, he was gone.

***

"Slim!" Brian called out, giving me a hearty bear hug, and pulling me away from my thoughts about the previous evening with Matt. "Hope I didn't keep you waiting long?"

"No, not at all."

"Good, let's get this show on the road and then we will meet my dad for lunch. How does that sound?"

"Perfect."

Brian was the ideal tour guide as he showed me the beautiful offices of the Cort Group, and pointed out, rather enthusiastically, I might add, a very cheap cafeteria with the "best muffins in the world" on 59th street, the closest subway station to the office tower, and finally the *piece de resistance* (his words, not mine), the flagship Apple Store at the base of the building, whose entrance is a glass cube reminiscent of the Louvre Pyramid. After the whirlwind tour, Brian and I walked to lunch and he filled me in on what life was like at the small elite firm. He said it could be "intense" at times, but he swore that it had a "great familial culture" and "very competent people" that made it worthwhile. He said that the pro of working for the Cort Group was access to senior management, not a lot of bureaucracy, fast decision-making, and better pay. He emphasized that while I might find good pay at a larger firm, as a junior employee, I would be a *small fish, in a big pond*, and that I most *assuredly* would miss out.

We arrived at Opia, a modern French bistro, on East 57th, that Brian told me was one of his dad's favorite lunch spots near the office when he was in town. The atmosphere was casual with an elegant vibe, and the menu was extensive with lots of choices.

As I studied the menu, I heard a familiar masculine laugh, "I'll save you time Samantha, order the Niçoise Salad, it's the best you'll ever have," said Mr. Cort, coming over to the table and giving me a hug when I stood to greet him.

For the next two hours, Brian and his dad painted me a picture of what life would be like at the Cort Group. They told me that their success was derived from a "total-control" approach.

"What do you mean by total-control *exactly*?" I asked as I popped a cherry tomato into my mouth.

"We do everything in-house for our clients with the help of our legal and tax group. We don't want to count on a third party doing anything," Mr. Cort replied. "In addition to investing client assets, we also take care of the less glamorous needs, such as managing their trust and estate plans, tax plans, insurance needs and philanthropic efforts. By doing this, we control the entire process from beginning to end."

"What about corporate clients?" I inquired.

"That conversation is better to have with Matt as that's his area of expertise," Mr. Cort stated. "In my opinion, the Cort Group is first and foremost a family-centered business serving the needs of one's family, but Matt persuaded me to take on a few institutional clients in recent years and it has worked out well."

Brian added, "For most of the Cort Group's history we advised and managed about one hundred high net-worth individual and family accounts totaling an estimated $6.9 billion with approximately fifty employees. When we opened the New York office, we expanded our services to provide corporate advisory and asset management services to clients around the world, bringing us up to almost two hundred accounts totaling an estimated $12.2 billion, and slightly over one hundred employees."

"Advisory is our key strength Samantha," Mr. Cort stressed, "whether for individuals, families, or institutions. We are a growing firm, with good people, low turnover, much better job security, and definitely a better lifestyle then you will find at a large firm, however it's a tough business and you'll be swimming with sharks. I don't want to gloss over the fact that it can be high pressure, tight deadlines and long hours."

"I appreciate your honesty Mr. Cort and I know what I'm getting into if I go into this line of work." I said genuinely, brushing a stray hair behind my ear. "I have just one more question, why do you want me?"

"Samantha, that's a silly question," he admonished lightly. "Don't you know by now that you are like a member of the family to us, and the same holds true for your brother, Peter. You embody the best of everything we strive for when we look for top talent—character, integrity, passion. You, of all people, deserve to succeed and flourish. If I can help with your career and look out for you along the way, it would give me great satisfaction."

"Thank you, Mr. Cort, that's very kind of you." I said gratefully, blushing slightly from his praise. "You've given me a lot to think about. Could I let you know my decision next week?"

"That's fine, Samantha," he said with a warm smile, then he nodded his head in Brian's direction and got up from the table mumbling something about a meeting that he was late for. We made plans to talk on the phone the next week and said good-bye.

I took a last sip of iced tea while Brian paid the bill. "Shall we?" he asked, getting up from the table and reaching out his hand to escort me from the restaurant.

Brian and I lingered on 57th for a few more minutes carrying on like old friends, and then he grasped my hand again and lifted it to his lips, "It was good seeing you Slim and I hope you decide to accept the job."

"Thanks Brian, you've given me a lot to consider."

"I should go Slim, but how about dinner next week?"

"I would like that, Brian," I answered truthfully.

"Great!" Brian smiled broadly, giving me a wink. "I'll call you next week to arrange it."

Returning his sunny smile, I watched Brian walk back towards his office. When he was finally out of sight, I turned, walking briskly in the opposite direction. Weaving in and out among people on the crowded sidewalk, my smile started to fade, and I wondered if socializing with Matt and Brian again was a good idea. Illogically, my mood darkened, and I began to panic. I was suddenly flooded with memories of that magical summer, and for a brief second, I could almost feel Matt's lips and the spray of saltwater on my face. But then just as forcibly, I was confronted with the sick twisted images that followed from its wake, and I wondered for the umpteenth time if Matt, Brian, and I could ever truly be friends again?

Certainly, it seemed like we had all moved past it and in the grand scheme of things. I felt almost ridiculous, for making so much out of it. Really it was insignificant, nothing more than puppy love and high school angst. But deep within my core, I knew that was not entirely true and just because we were young at the time did not diminish that it wasn't important.

I shook my head in a final attempt to forget the past. It was time to focus on the future, and what lay ahead.

Chapter 14: The 'Cortship' blossoms – July 2005

Heather, Ryan, Matt and I made our way through the crowded dance floor at Avalon, a popular live music nightclub in Boston, to see one of our favorite band's perform. The club smelled of stale beer, bad cologne, and body odor, but when Coldplay moved to the edge of the stage to play an acoustic version of the song *A Rush of Blood to the Head*, Heather and I screamed in delight, bumping and grinding to the music. Every so often I looked up, surprised to find Matt watching me and I smiled back shyly. He returned my smile, and he would occasionally lean into me to say something, brushing up against me, and putting his hand on my back or hip. Throughout the evening, our eyes were on each other nearly all the time. I felt a surge of confidence that maybe Matt was developing feelings for me, like I had for him.

After the concert was over, I followed Matt as he took my hand and led me through the glow stick waving, spiky haired, tight T-shirt wearing crowd. Once outside, the sticky-thick humid July air assaulted us, and Matt abruptly let go of my hand as Heather and Ryan joined us. I wiped the beads of sweat away from my forehead and listened to the slap of our feet as we walked by the bars on Lansdowne Street in the direction of the lot where Matt had parked the Range Rover.

"What's the deal with you and my brother?" Heather asked in a low voice coming up to stand next to me.

I started to walk along side of her. "Which one, Brian or Matt?" I asked innocently.

"Come on, don't play dumb with me. You know damn well, that I mean Matt!" she said raising her voice. "You guys couldn't keep your eyes off each other tonight, and what's with all the whispering, giggling, and touching. Are you hooking up with him?"

I tensed slightly and shook my head. Of course not, Heather and could you please lower your voice before someone hears you?" I pleaded.

Before she could respond, Ryan, who stood waiting in an incredibly long line for late night pizza with Matt, called out, "Anyone want a slice?"

"I'll take a spring water," Heather said.

We got to where they were standing in line. "Make that two," I added.

The boys looked over at us and Heather threw her arms around her brother's neck. "Bet you're happy, Matt, that you joined us for the concert!" Heather said smugly. "I told you it would be awesome!"

Matt rolled his eyes. "Yeah, right. Because I love armpits in my mouth, people spilling drinks all over me, and being dry humped from behind."

"You're too much!" Heather said exasperated, flicking her hair over her shoulder, and stomping away from him. It's Friday night, time to chill out and have some fun. Could you quit being an old grouch for 5-minutes?

He raised an eyebrow at her. "I'm the old one, huh? Well, this old man was out of bed at 5:00 a.m. running by 5:15, and in the office by 7:00 a.m. You were still sleeping. When exactly did you wake up? Noon?"

"What's your point Matt?" Heather asked defensively. "Are you trying to call me lazy, just because I'm enjoying my summer vacation. Don't blame me for your grueling work schedule. Not to mention the outrageous amount of time that you and Sam spend on the water practicing for that damn boat race. I think you're both *banana sandwiches* for doing it!"

"Banana what?" I screeched. "Hey, don't pull me into this argument."

After the guys got their pizza, we crossed the road to the parking lot and made our way to Matt's car while brother and sister continued to argue. "Ladies first," he said opening the passenger door for me. Then he looked over his shoulder at Heather, "please try not to throw up in this car too?"

"With your attitude, you're lucky I don't vomit all over you or better yet all over your precious boat equipment and foul-weather gear," she yelled back. "I mean really Matt, could this car be anymore stuffed?"

"Heather, stop bickering with your brother." Ryan interrupted. "I swear you both sound like an old married couple."

Heather smiled innocently at Ryan, and then turned her attention to Matt and me, while she buckled her seat belt. "Well, maybe we *sound* like a married couple, but believe me if anyone *acts* like a couple around here - it is Matt and Sammy. Are you two dating?" she asked suspiciously, her eyes traveling brazenly between the two of us.

Closing my eyes and taking a deep breath, I nervously glanced at Matt, who shot his sister a warning look in the rear-view mirror but unphased. He put the car in reverse and pulled out his wallet to pay the parking attendant.

Undeterred, Heather grimaced and pressed on. "So, what's going *on?*"

Pissed, I pursed my lips and turned to her. "You caught us Heather. We were fucking in the bathroom tonight, and it was hot!" I said sarcastically, casting her a sharp glare. "Satisfied?"

Heather leaned over in her seat, bursting into uncontrollable laughter, and before I knew it everyone in the car was laughing hard.

"You are so full of shit Sammy. That's hilarious!" Heather scoffed, between giggles, tears streaming down her face.

Suddenly, I stopped laughing, and was irritated. *Why was it so funny? Was it really that outrageous to think of Matt and me together like that?* Sitting back, I regarded everyone for a moment, then without thinking, I blurted out, "It's really not that funny! It could have happened."

The laughter abruptly stopped, and an awkward lull followed. Well, it felt awkward to me as I sat there embarrassed, biting my lip. I cringed slightly, knowing that I had really screwed up. I may not have drunkenly kissed Matt and shown him my tits this time, but I think on some level that in my outburst; I may have unwittingly confessed my desire for him, and if that was truly the case, then *this* was infinitely worse. "I'm just joking," I said quietly, attempting to lighten the mood and hoping that no one noticed the slight tremor in my voice.

"We know," Heather responded kindly, and in a very un-Heather like fashion, she asked Ryan if he knew the score of the Red Sox game. I was thankful for the change in subject and sat quietly for the rest of the ride home, looking out the window, while the others discussed baseball.

It was almost 3:00 a.m., when we pulled up in front of the Corts' house. I was about to step out of the car, when Matt reached out to me. "Could we talk for a minute?" Then he turned to Heather and Ryan, and told them to go ahead without us, and that we would be there soon.

He continued to hold my hand, his thumb stroking my palm, and my heart hammered erratically from his gentle touch. It was a long moment before he spoke, and when he did his voice was hoarse. "Sam, I need to know if something is going on between you and my brother?"

"What?" I gaped.

"It's obvious that Brian has feelings for you, and if there is a chance that you could reciprocate those feelings, I need to know now."

"Why?" I asked, turning my head to see him.

He leaned towards me. "Because, I want to kiss you, it's all I've been able to think about." He said softly, his fingers reaching out to brush a stray piece of hair from my eyes.

His words sent a thrill through my entire body and I took a deep breath to steady myself. "Oh," I said unevenly. I couldn't believe how nervous and excited I felt. *Was this really happening?*

"Sam?" he questioned, his voice low and demanding.

"Um," I stuttered. "I – I don't want to hurt Brian, and…"

"And what?" he demanded. "Say it Sam?"

"I think the world of him, but…"

"Yes?"

I felt scared and vulnerable, but I knew that I could not conceal the truth any longer and after a lifetime of hiding my true feelings, I didn't want to hide anymore. So, I met his gaze and put everything on the line. "I don't feel for Brian, what I feel for you."

With those words, Matt took me in his arms and crashed his lips against mine. He kissed me long and hard, and I thought I was going to melt into a puddle of goo on the floor. My hands trembled as I placed them on his chest and I moaned softly when his tongue slipped into my mouth, tasting me for the first time. I had kissed a few boys before, but no one had ever made me feel like this. I had never felt anything as intimate as Matt's lips fully against me, and like a drug, I was desperate and hungry for more.

***

The month of July and the days leading up to the Berringer Bowl race were among the happiest of my life. Matt and I spent every free moment together, and when we were not training with the crew, we would stare adoringly into each other's eyes, hold hands, and kiss for hours. I never wanted it to end.

I thought I knew everything there was to know about Matt, after all I had grown up around him, and was practically a member of his family, but I was wrong, because there was still so much new information to learn about him. In those hot summer days, we talked and talked. He opened up about his fear of failure, his restlessness, and his need for control. And I shared with him my fear of not getting into Stanford, my alarm over being too timid and reserved, and my desire to become more independent and assertive.

We also laughed and joked, and I saw a lighthearted side to him that he seldom showed me before. We were inseparable, and on the few occasions that we were not together, I thought about him nearly constantly. The real Matthew Cort was so much better than my schoolgirl crush, and much better than any fantasy I had, about him. He was perfect and I was falling head over heels in love with him.

Chapter 15: A Friendship Rekindled – June 2013

I walked into the *happenings* at the Standard Grill in the meatpacking district at 7:30 p.m. sharp on Friday night to meet Heather for dinner and drinks. The place was crowded, and the front café looked more like a pickup scene, rather than a place to be eat. Not exactly the quiet, intimate spot that I had imagined for our first outing together after eight years.

I glanced around the crowded bar, and after a few minutes of searching, I spotted her and heard her effusive laughter. She was at the bar, champagne in one perfectly manicured hand, an oyster in the other, surrounded by a group of men who seemed to be hanging on her every word, and I realized that Heather was still the *good-time girl*, very little had changed on that front.

When I made my way over to her spot, she hugged me tightly, and enthusiastically introduced me to the group of five men that she was socializing with. The most outspoken among them, Alberto, a polished and urban looking dark-haired gentleman, in his early thirties (give or take a few years), eagerly clasped my hand and handed me a glass of champagne. His friend, Isaac, stood up from the bar and kindly offered me his seat, which I happily accepted. We drank and laughed with them until our table was ready, and politely refused all offers "to go back to their place" after dinner.

Once seated in the cozy main dining room, I took the time to carefully examine Heather. Although I had just seen her two weeks ago in London, the experience of seeing all the Corts again had been so jarring and overwhelming that I had not savored the moment to actually "see" her. Heather looked and acted exactly as I remembered, still a beautiful, blonde, blue-eyed tornado of energy, but the years had transformed her, and somehow, if possible, she was more exquisite and even more confident than I had recalled.

We ordered our meals and started to get reacquainted again. It was such a long time since we'd spoken, but we picked up easily right where we left off. Heather told me about her years studying both Fashion Merchandising and Fashion Design at the

San Francisco Academy of Art. After graduating from school, Heather did a short stint as an intern at Calvin Klein in New York; but then moved back to California when she got her first job with designer Richard Tyler in LA, followed by her second job working for designer Tom Ford, also based in LA. After 6+ years in California, Heather landed her dream job as a fashion buyer for Barneys, and subsequently moved back to the East Coast a little over a year ago.

The server had just brought our salads to the table and I stabbed a tomato with my fork when Heather launched into her attack and allowed the floodgates to open. She expressed her disappointment with me for blowing her off, when I decided "at the very last second" not to attend Stanford. She went on to ream me for the better half of an hour about my "utter selfishness" and although she understood that I needed to get away from her overzealous brothers and their "sick, twisted game of tug of war with me," that my behavior was insensitive and that after being my best friend for over a decade, that she deserved better.

I couldn't dispute her claims, so I groveled and apologized profusely, however in my defense, I explained to her my desperate need to get away from her *larger than life* family and that although I loved her, that I had needed space and distance to grow up and find my own identity, away from them. I described in great detail, my struggles with getting over my love-hate feelings for Matt, and my guilt for not returning Brian's strong romantic feelings.

"Well, that's not exactly accurate Sam, is it?" she questioned, furrowing her brow.

"What do you mean?" I asked, raising my brow at her, slightly perplexed by her statement.

"For God's sake, Sammy, you hooked up with Brian at our senior prom, so obviously you shared some of his romantic feelings." Heather said unsympathetically, a look of censorship clear on her face. "When I heard about it, I was humiliated and embarrassed for you. I mean, how could you be with both of them and in the span of the same eleven-month period, no less? It was disgusting!"

I cringed at the revulsion, unmistakable in her tone and stared open-mouthed at her, stunned. I couldn't blame her for thinking harshly of me, because what she described was something right out of an episode of *Days of Our Lives* or a Lifetime movie of the week special. It reeked of tabloid talks shows and trashy gossip magazines, and it was sordid, but above all else, it was *false - not* true.

"Heather, let me stop you right there, because you seem to be under the false impression that I had sex with Brian."

Heather jutted out her chin, appraising me carefully. "Well, didn't you?" she accused.

I lifted my eyes to her and took a long sip of my wine. "I never had sex with Brian." I stated firmly, emphasizing each word. "Why would you think that?"

"Well, I'll be damned," she whispered almost to herself. "Let's order another bottle of wine, shall we?"

Several glasses later, she explained in painstaking detail, a fight that transpired between Matt and Brian, that caused her to think that I had slept with not one, but two of her brothers, and resulted in one black eye, one broken toe, two bruised egos, and two brothers not talking to each other for over a year.

I was floored by her admission and filled with righteous anger. "What *exactly* did Brian say to Matt?"

Heather shifted uneasily in her seat, drumming her fingers on the table. "It's not what he said, it's more what he didn't say," she explained.

"Which was *what* exactly?"

"Sam, it was a long time ago. Do you really think I remember it word for word?" she snapped, obviously getting annoyed by my questions.

Equally annoyed, I glared at her. "I have a right to know," I groaned. "Please tell me what Brian said or didn't say to make you and Matt believe that I had sex with him?"

Heather shrugged and then looked down at the table, it was obvious that she was feeling more than a little embarrassed for Brian and his disgraceful behavior. "Oh, I don't know.

Basically, I think it was something like him bragging about spending the night with you during our senior prom, and how you hated Matt."

"Did Brian actually say that we had sex?"

"I don't think he said it in those words, but he definitely insinuated it."

"I see."

"Please don't be angry with Brian," she pleaded. "It was a long time ago and he was just a dumb college kid with a bruised ego and a broken heart."

Nervously, I tapped my fingers against my empty wine glass. "Can I ask you just one more question?"

"Shoot? What is it Sam?"

"When was the fight?"

Heather smirked slightly. "It was the morning of our high school graduation. You probably didn't notice it, but Brian wore sunglasses during the ceremony to hide his black eye."

I smirked back at Heather, but on the inside, I was struggling. I felt nauseous as a tight knot of resentment pulled at my stomach. I remembered the memory of our graduation, and with stunning, vivid details I recalled how cold and distant Matt was as I said good-bye to him and his family, and my hurt at what I perceived to be his indifference.

Knowing the truth of what happened between Matt and Brian the morning of my graduation, would have offered some clarity. In the grand scheme of things, it would not have changed the events of that summer, nor my senior year, nor me moving to London the day after graduation. But it may have helped me to understand Matt's perspective and changed my opinion about him and what happened when we exchanged our final goodbye on that fateful afternoon eight years ago. Suddenly I felt cheated, because if I had known; it could have eased the overwhelming sense of regret that had consumed me year after year, for putting myself in the vulnerable position of loving him to begin with.

"Anyway," Heather said, refilling my wineglass. She sounded uncomfortable and cleared her throat. "It was a long time ago, let's forget it and move on."

"I'll drink to that!" I said, raising and clinking my wineglass against hers.

Chapter 16: Berringer Bowl – July 2005

The race started at about 7:00 p.m. on the third Friday in July, with fifty or more sleek racing crafts working their way across the bay, eleven of which were competing against us in the A class. The wind that warm summer evening was right behind us. So, we had our colorful kite-like sails called spinnakers, or what Heather affectionately dubbed "thong underwear" shaped sails, out in front as we sailed downwind. It was a beautiful view, and fun and exhilarating to be part of the action.

While the winds were light the competition wasn't. The Sailfish II led by Tanner Harrington, and three other boats were neck and neck with us through the first turning mark outside Boston Harbor. Soon after that, the race started to thin out and we lost track of them as the skies darkened. I watched with great interest as Matt and the crew measured with instruments the Cortship's performance in the wind and on the racecourse. I remembered Matt telling me over and over again, "To win races, especially overnight in the dark, your boat handling must be second nature, your boat speed second to none, and you must learn to be an instrument guy or gal, it's the only way to judge an accurate performance."

"Are you enjoying your first overnight race?" Stacy asked. Stacy Anderson was the only other female crewmember on board the Cortship. She was a wisecracking, but good-natured girl. She had short blonde hair, freckles, and brown eyes. We quickly became friends during the water practices and Wednesday night boat races leading up to the race. Stacy and her boyfriend, John Mead, had graduated high school with Matt, and they were now entering their last year at Boston University. They both sailed regularly with Matt and this was their third time competing in the Berringer Bowl on board the Cortship. Both loved the challenge of sailing and the camaraderie of a team sport, and they "understood boating" which according to Matt was what you needed to race competitively. I sometimes argued this point with Matt, which drove him crazy.

"Don't you think someone who is athletic could master boating and race competitively?" I asked.

"No," he answered dryly.

"Well, why not?"

"Sure, you need to be athletic Sam, but that's not enough to be good. Look at Brian, he is one of the most athletic people I know, but he's an awful sailor. Sailing is a deeply complex and sophisticated sport. If you want to be good and race competitively, you need to understand it first."

"So, are you saying, because I'm fairly athletic, if I take the time to understand boating, I could master it?"

He laughed so hard, that his eyes began to water. Then he ruffled my hair like a child. "You're so cute Sam! But, the good thing about sailing is that it's not an activity that can easily be mastered, that's the fun and challenge of it."

I gave him an angry look and wanted to kill him for laughing so hard at me.

Don't be angry Sam - believe me when I say that understanding is what is needed to race competitively. The people who only think about speed don't get it. Learn the skills of reading wind shifts, and the patience of sailboat racing tactics and you'll be a great sailor one day."

Stacy was looking at me and waiting for my answer. "It's been incredible so far, I just hope I've been helpful enough," I replied.

"You're doing great and you've learned to be safe and handy on a boat. This can only come when you jump in with two feet like you have. You're on your way, Samantha!"

I smiled at Stacy. "Thanks. As long as we finish ahead of the Sailfish II, I will be happy. I didn't tell Matt, because he would go ballistic, but I ran into Tanner yesterday. He gave me a hard time about choosing the *wrong* boat to crew on and he was a real cocky SOB about it."

Stacy rolled her eyes. "Oh Sam, like any of us would be surprised by that! Tanner has never been beat before, and this race will be no different. Just, because his daddy got him a new shiny boat, doesn't mean he will sail any better on it. You know the joke about the Sailfish crew, right?

"No, what?"

"That they'll be drunk off their asses by the time it's dark out!" Stacy smirked, grinning broadly for being the first to share this.

"It wouldn't surprise me if that is true with those morons!"

"Morons yes, but probably not enough common sense to wait to be intoxicated until they reach Provincetown."

"You think?" I asked, and we both erupted into laugher.

Conditions on the course were in a constant state of change. The wind never steadied for longer than ten minutes nor did the velocity ever even out, always rising or falling and not by just a few tenths either. Around 2:00 a.m. the rain showers began, then a little later lightening, showers, some of which brought us a thorough soaking and rocked the boat around roughly. But the most terrorizing moment of all came at about 3:00 a.m., when the engine failed, and the lights and gauges went out. We had to sail invisible for a while, which was downright terrifying.

I watched with admiration as Matt and some of the more experienced crewmembers worked in close-knit harmony through the rain filled slog jumping the battery and getting the engine to power back up. I respected their intense focus and brute-like strength as they kept the Cortship moving efficiently through the dark.

"I guess you were right, the ocean and wind cannot be predicted," I said, bringing Matt a bottle of water.

"Thanks," Matt said. "Are you doing okay?"

"I liked it better when we sailed into the sunset under cloudless starlit skies," I smirked, only half jesting. "What would you have done if the engine didn't come back on?"

"Don't worry Sam, we have a backup generator so everything would have been fine. I promise you that it will be toasty and warm before you know it," Matt whispered in my ear, giving me a little squeeze. "Go inside and take a nap; no need to continue to get soaked with us."

"I'm okay," I protested.

"You're so stubborn," Matt said, swatting me on the behind. "Hey Sam, on Sunday, most of the crew plans to take the fast ferry from Provincetown to Boston, but I'm going to stay a few days to have the engine tested. Do you want to stay with me?"

"Nothing could tear me away from you," I whispered, shooting him a half smile before we both pulled away and resumed our positions on the boat.

The weather cleared, and sometime after dawn we all pulled off our foul-weather gear. We felt a tiny puff of wind and through the faint haze of an early Saturday morning; it began to occur to us that the boat might have done well as we rounded the large bell buoy outside of Provincetown harbor to come in first out of eleven boats.

It was an incredibly tense, yet serene experience. I felt hugely proud to be part of an amazing crew that could win and have fun together. That alone was unforgettable. We all started to laugh and hug, and I was filled with so much emotion and relief that I got all choked up. When I spotted Matt coming towards me; salty and joyous, a huge grin spread over his perfect features, and it was one of my favorite moments.

"Breathe Sam," he laughed, radiating joy. Then he grabbed me tenderly and swung me happily around. "We won!"

I nodded, flushed and happy, and released the stress that I had been holding all night long.

He held me close, burying his face in my hair. "Look at you, sailing on the open water and winning already! We are on our way, baby!"

Chapter 17: Sunday Brunch – June 2013

I heard a faint buzzing from far away and rolled onto my back clutching the pillow over my head. If I waited long enough, maybe the sound would go away. Just as my eyes closed again, the alarm on my iPhone went off. It was 6:45 a.m. Sunday morning and I had promised Matt that I would run with him in fifteen minutes. I heard the buzzing again, but this time I couldn't ignore it, because I had figured out the source of it.

I stood up, and walked to the front door, hitting the buzzer. "Hello?"

"There is a Matt Cort here to see you."

"Yes, please send him up."

Carefully, I adjusted my tank top and boy shorts, wondering if I had time to go to the bathroom to put on my bathrobe, and properly brush my hair and teeth, before he arrived. But then I heard a "rat-a-tat" at the door and knew that my time was up. Quickly, I ran my hands through my messy bedroom hair in an attempt to even it out. Then, straightening my posture, I opened the door. When he walked in, he was the epitome of perfect male athleticism and strength, like a fitness model from the pages of Men's Health. I let my eyes linger on the muscles of his forearms for a fraction longer than necessary, and when I re-gained my focus, our eyes met. But I wasn't embarrassed from being caught ogling him. What got under my skin was that he smirked a little, and seemed overly cheerful and energetic, like he had been wide-awake for hours and it wasn't even seven yet.

"You're early," I grumbled.

"And good morning to you too, little Miss Sunshine," said Matt, walking past me and putting his gym bag on the floor. Then he walked over to the kitchen and placed a grocery bag on the counter.

"What's that?" I asked. "I thought we were going to brunch later?"

"We are, but you still need to hydrate and have something in your stomach until then," Matt answered dumping the contents of the bag onto the counter. He had brought bananas, four bottles of Gatorade, six bottles of water, and sun block.

"You don't miss a thing, do you?"

He nodded and winked. "Glad that you haven't forgotten, Sam."

I smiled and rubbed my hands together. "I better get dressed."

"Don't get dressed on my account," he whistled suggestively eyeing my skimpy tank top and boy shorts that I wore to bed.

My heart started to pound. "Get your mind out of the gutter, Cort!"

I laughed and turned to leave, waving at him quickly. "I'm going to change now, so please be quiet, because Pete is still sleeping."

"I'll be as quiet as a mouse," he said in a low voice, grinning.

I smiled again, but this time he didn't see me as I shut the bedroom door to get ready. *Matthew Cort was going to be the death of me.*

***

We jogged Central Park Drive, which offered both hilly and flat terrain and circled the entire park. It was crowded with other runners, cyclists, skaters, and pedestrians, but at least it was closed to traffic on the weekends. We had gotten most of the hills out of the way, so the rest of the run was flat surfaces and easy footing, which I was happy about, because my body was sticky with sweat and I was exhausted already. Of course, Matt was a good distraction, as I watched him pour yet another bottle of water (now I understood his need for so many bottles of water and Gatorade) down his body. His hair was damp from sweat and his shorts were now drenched from the bottle of water that was dripping down his rear. *Yummy ... what a view, a quarter could easily bounce off that ass!*

"We've done over six miles, so how about we cool down and walk back to Peter's now," he suggested.

"Um-sure," I mumbled, abruptly pulling my gaze from his ass, and trying to hide my guilty expression, as I walked over to where he stood and stretched.

"You're still a fast runner," he finally said, looking into my eyes, while moving his neck slowly back and forth and cracking his back.

"I guess," I muttered without further comment, while going into a downward facing dog pose, which was my first stretch in my post-run yoga sequence.

"What other stretches do you usually do after running?" he asked, grinning, coming up to stand very close to me and doing a downward facing dog pose next to me.

Distracted by his close proximity, I stumbled unexpectedly, and he caught me. "Are you okay?"

"Yes," I laughed nervously, shaking my head. I looked around the park and tried to mentally get back into my yoga stretches. "I usually do a quad stretch, followed by a fallen warrior pose, and then hamstrings. When I do these stretches, I feel like it really helps loosen and strengthen my tight muscles."

"It sounds like a good healthy way to keep a runner's high going all day long." Matt joked, giving me a steamy look. "Show me your stretches and I'll show you mine, Sam." He laughed and I felt his warm breath tickle my neck.

"You are such a troublemaker," I joked in return, gently punching him in his hard stomach. "Come on, that's enough stretching. Let's go."

***

Peter was notably absent from the apartment when we returned to shower and I did not think it was a good idea to be alone with Matt, so I rushed to get ready, politely but as fast as was humanly possible. Soon after, we cabbed it to the village for brunch. "Look at that line! We're never going to eat." I pouted, getting out of the cab, and taking my place in the long line in front of Café Mogador, a Mediterranean-inspired East Village joint that Matt claimed was the best brunch spot in all of New York City.

"Hungry, eh?" Matt said coming to join me after paying the cab fare. "I told you that you should have eaten a banana earlier." He scolded playfully, while shaking his head, and giving me an indulgent smile, like I was a child who needed to be coddled. Then he held out his hand and led me past the long line. "Just stick with me kid and we'll be seated before you can count to ten."

Sure, enough Matt was true to his word, and we bypassed the immediately jealous crowd, who gave us disdainful stares as we glided by like rock stars and were seated at a comfortable corner table in less than five minutes.

"How'd you do that?" I asked, amazed.

He shrugged. "I have my methods."

Over coffee, blood-orange mimosas, and savory goat cheese, tomato, and spinach omelets, Matt went into business mode. He talked to me about the independent, hands-on environment of the Cort Group and his wish to maintain the small firm environment while still growing the business. He confided his dad's fears about becoming more institutionalized and his own conflicts on how to keep the small feel while still expanding and growing the corporate accounts. I tried to concentrate on what he was saying, but my mind kept slipping to my conversation with Heather about Matt and Brian's fight on my high school graduation and I struggled on whether I should bring the topic up or not.

"Am I boring you?" he asked bluntly bringing me back to the present conversation.

"Of course not," I lied. "You were talking about institutional clients. Please continue…"

I directed my full attention to Matt as he went on to describe the Cort Group's institutional clients who were mostly established small to middle market companies with proven business models and stable cash flows. The topic was interesting, but my mind kept wandering and I had to focus twice as hard to keep up with what he was saying.

"Have you heard a word I've said to you?" Matt asked pointedly, fixing me with a look that was part irritated, part bemused.

"I'm sorry," I said uneasily. "I know that I've been distracted."

"Yeah, you've been far away all morning. What's troubling you Sam?"

"Just forget it Matt. It's nothing really."

"Obviously Sam, something is bothering you. What is it?"

I was embarrassed to bring it up, and vehemently hoped that I wasn't blushing, which was an awkward trait that I used to do quite regularly, but since college, it was a rare occurrence for me to do it anymore. "I feel foolish bringing it up," I whispered.

"You have nothing to feel foolish about," he answered, waiting for me to continue. "What is it?"

"I had dinner with Heather on Friday night," I said quietly, pushing my eggs around my plate.

"I know. You mentioned that you were seeing Heather Friday night, and an old boyfriend last night. How was it?"

"Which?"

"Both?"

I shot a dirty look at Matt. "Both were fine. Could you stop and just listen."

Matt turned to me and let out a deep sigh. "I'm listening."

"The conversation with Heather was-" I dropped my fork and looked directly at him, "Enlightening."

"How so?" he asked, confused.

I let me eyes drop to my hands and I fidgeted with my napkin. "She told me about the fight that you and Brian had the morning of my high school graduation."

I watched him take a sip of his coffee and then he looked at me before taking another bite of his omelet. "And?"

"I know it was a long time ago Matt, and I'm sorry to bring it up now." I laughed a little, trying to ease the tension that I heard in my voice. "But I wanted to tell you something…"

He wiped his mouth, placing his napkin on the table. "I'm listening."

"Like I said, it was a long time ago, and I know that what I have to say doesn't make a difference anymore, but still you should know the truth…"

"Know what?" he demanded. "Tell me."

I sighed and closed my eyes briefly. "I think you may have been under the wrong impression that something happened between Brian and me during the night of my senior prom." I stated uncomfortably, swallowing a large sip of mimosa. "Anyway, I just wanted to set the record straight, and let you know that nothing ever happened between us."

I could feel him watching me closely as I took another sip of mimosa and busied myself with pushing food around my plate and looking around the restaurant, at everything, but him.

"Thank you for telling me, Sam," he said gently, pulling my chin up with his index finger. He smiled at me tenderly, and looked, to be honest, relieved. "I cannot tell you how happy I am to hear that," he acknowledged, leaning back in his chair. "And now that I know, I'm going to kick Brian's ass."

I looked up at him and panicked. "I don't want you to fight with your brother over this. Do you promise to let me handle it?"

He stared at me with a clenched jaw. His expression was tight but restrained. Then his eyes softened, and he leaned in closer. "Okay, Sam, I promise not to kick his ass, but only if you promise me something in return?"

"What?" I asked, watching him through narrowed eyes.

"I want you to trust me again. Do you think you could try?" he asked, his voice strained and full of longing, his eyes hopeful, his gaze intense.

"Oh," I said, confused by how vulnerable and sincere he seemed, but fearful of letting down my guard around him. I felt scared, knowing that the cost of trusting him again; I could get hurt. I had no idea what to say to him. Finally, I pushed away my jarring emotions, and decided to take a leap of faith. I reached for his hand across the table. "I don't know, Matt. I can't just snap my fingers and be ready. It will take time."

"Of course, I'm well aware that it will take time, Sam." He leaned forward and tucked a strand of hair behind my ear. "I'm willing to wait until you're ready."

"Um... I suppose I could try," I admitted softly, shifting in my seat, while firmly trying to ignore the stirring of hope that was quickly sprouting up in my chest. "Let's just take it one day at a time and see what happens."

Squeezing my hand, he raised my hand to his lips and kissed it softly. "One day at a time," he agreed, fixing me with a knowing smile.

Chapter 18: Provincetown, Cape Cod – July to August 2005

Our kisses were frenzied as we fumbled for the room key. We had checked into the Provincetown Inn with the rest of the crew earlier that morning after sharing a few rounds of celebratory Dark 'n' Stormy's. After a night spent racing on the water, everyone was dead on their feet and wanted to sleep for a few hours. After we slept, we all had plans to meet up at the Beringer Bowl Saturday nights regatta party that was the highlight of the weekend at the Inn for all of the sailors who had participated in the race.

I was a little lightheaded, whether from the Dark n' Stormy's, or lack of sleep or Matt's expert lips, I wasn't sure. I couldn't keep my hands off him as we kissed and groped there, salty and sweaty, on the doorstep. Finally, the door was opened, and we stumbled our way into the room. Then Matt had me by the hand and pulled me on top of him on the bed, and we started kissing. He pressed his muscled body against mine until I thought I would explode when he pulled away and asked, "Are you drunk?"

I shook my head and touched my lips to his until we were kissing again and again. My movements became frantic and I panted with desire as I tugged at his shirt. But he was unhurried. He took his time, kissing me firmly, but leisurely. Then he exhaled slowly, very slowly, and pulled back to look at me.

"Is this alright?" He whispered.

I nodded, breathless.

"If you want to stop, just tell me Sam."

I stared at him, smiling shyly, and then I kissed him, wrapping my hands around his neck. "I want you Matt…" Hurry, and put on a condom.

We had sex all morning and afternoon. It was my first time, so I was scared about the potential for pain and nervous about my inexperience. I didn't know what to expect, but Matt was perfect. He was romantic, considerate, confident, and he made me feel cherished and desired. As the afternoon wore on, he became more aggressive, and I became more assertive, and the sex became hotter and better than I ever could have imagined in my wildest dreams. Matt had skills! He brought me to an orgasm multiple times, and afterwards, I fell asleep, entwined in his arms, sated and happy. My last conscious thought before drifting to sleep, was that I was madly in love with him and that I never wanted to let him go.

***

When we arrived at the Inn's manicured lawn area for the regatta party, we were immediately treated to beautiful views of Provincetown and Cape Cod Bay. The band was playing Bob Dylan music and the aroma of barbecue food wafted in the warm summer breeze. It was noisy and crowded with young and old sailors alike, but I was unable to concentrate on anything, but Matt's touch. He was slowly driving me insane with his arm around my waist and his lips on my neck. Then he trailed his hand deliberately from my waist down to my behind, gradually putting his hand in my back pocket and stroking my backside with his thumb.

His touch sent shivers down my spine and I gazed at him with darkened eyes. I could hardly contain myself. I had never been so aroused before and I was eager to go back to our room to continue our lovemaking.

But before I could suggest returning to the room, Stacy Anderson and her boyfriend, John Mead came over with a round of shots. Followed by the rest of our five-man crew, which included three guys that Matt, Stacy and John had graduated high school with as well as a medical student and a newly graduated architect, both of whom Matt had sailed with regularly, they were devoted sailors.

Still high from winning the race, the crew was in the mood to party! We celebrated with friends for quite some time, drinking beer after beer and swaying happily to the music. Everyone was having a good time and the atmosphere was spirited. After a few hours, our friends gradually peeled away, many wanting to head downtown to see the nightlife.

Moving away from Matt's hold, I excused myself to go inside and find the ladies room. A few minutes later, I was heading back towards the party when I heard a male voice say my name. "Samantha!" I turned to see Tanner Harrington with a group of guys by the bar. "I have been looking for you, beautiful. Come over and join us for a drink!"

"Hi Tanner." I smiled, coming over and leaning against the bar next to where he and his buddies stood. "Congratulations on coming in third. Thanks for the drink offer, but my friends our waiting for me outside."

"Yeah right, third, yippee for us!" he said rolling his eyes, his tone was sarcastic, and I could smell the alcohol on his breath. "How about you blow off your friends, beautiful. Come for a walk on the beach with me?"

I felt uneasy in his company and I looked around for help, but I didn't see anyone who I trusted to help. "Sorry Tanner, I can't. Matt is waiting for me." I mumbled. "I'll see you around."

"Matthew Cort?" He said coming to stand very close to me and pushing a stray piece of hair away from my face.

I immediately flinched at his intimate gesture and took a step back. "I think you've had too much to drink, Tanner. I have to go." But he put an arm on either side of me, trapping me somewhat against the bar.

"You know Matt isn't as great as everyone thinks," he slurred, his hot breath against my ear, making me feel uneasy.

"I know who Matt *is*. Now let me go Tanner?"

"I will beautiful, but only if you promise to go out with me on a date?"

I started to object, when I heard Matt's furious voice. "There you are, Sam. I've been looking for you."

Both men glowered at each other and Matt looked angry like he wanted to punch Tanner. "I suggest you take your hands off my girlfriend *now*?"

"I didn't realize you two were an item?" Tanner said snidely, dropping his arms from my side, and stepping aside.

Matt took my hand and pulled me into his embrace. "Well, now you know Tanner. So, stay away from her."

We started to walk away when Tanner's sour voice was suddenly behind us. "It's too bad that Matt has to go back to California in a few weeks, because we all know long-distance relationships don't work. Tough break! See you in September, beautiful!"

Matt turned his penetrating gaze on Tanner. "You want to take this outside you little fucker?"

"Sure, lead the way pretty boy!" Tanner snarled at Matt.

"Stop arguing with each other!" I shouted at them both, trying to defuse the confrontation, before someone got hurt. "Matt, please take me back to the room, *now*!" I begged, impatient to get out of there without a fight.

Tanner's friends came over and like me, they seemed anxious to avoid a fight. "Come on, Tanner, we are heading downtown for some action. Let's go!"

Tanner stood there for a minute and then did a strange curtsy-type thing – it sorts of looked like a mock salute to us. "Alright, I'm fucking drunk so I'll go with my boys. Later, sweet

Samantha," he muttered as he stumbled away from us with his friends.

"I would like to tear him apart!" Matt said, his tone glacial, as he strode in the direction where Tanner and his friends went. "No!" I pleaded, trying to block his path. "Please, Matt. I'm begging you to stop and calm down!"

Matt clenched his teeth together, his expression wild. Finally, he looked at me, and his expression softened. Then, resting his forehead against mine, he let out a strained breath of air. When he was calmer, he kissed my nose. "Ok. Let's go back to the room," he groaned against my lips.

***

Matt was in a foul mood and he moved with the determination and speed of a predator! Maybe I should have been scared, but all I could think about was how hot and sexy it was. The moment we entered our room, he walked over to me and pushed me up against the wall. I could feel his warm breath on my face as his tongue licked my lips and then he whispered, "It's time that I introduce you to wall sex." I felt faint, as his fingers caressed my breasts through my shirt and then in one swift motion, he took off my shirt and tossed it aside, followed by my bra. "You have perfect breasts," he murmured, cupping them in his hands, and then squeezing and sucking each hard nipple until I screamed in ecstasy.

He parted my mouth roughly with his tongue. Then his hand slid up to my skirt, lifting it, and shrugging it up until it settled around my waist. He stared at me with lust in his eyes, causing me to get so damn wet, that I thought I might convulse right there on the spot. I stood there naked in my damp white thong in front of him, my back pressed against the wall. "Fuck, you are beautiful! Ever since that night when you drunkenly stripped down to your underwear in front of me, I haven't been able to get you out of my head. Holy shit Sam, you take my breath away."

He tugged at the thin string of the thong and slipped his finger inside. My body ached desperately for his touch, and I spread my legs wider for him. He plunged his finger inside me thrusting back and forth. "You are so wet," he remarked, huskily, and that was my undoing, as I moaned his name as I came.

Breathless from my orgasm, my body slumped, and I thought my legs were going to buckle underneath me, but Matt had other plans for us. He held me up supporting my weight, while he unzipped his pants. He sheathed himself and lifted my legs up wrapping them around his hips as he plunged into me. With each thrust, I could hear the thud of my back against the wall punctuated by our loud moans until we both came in spectacular fashion.

***

During the weekend, we checked out Provincetown and spent five more unforgettable days sailing leisurely on the Cortship, stopping every day in a cute, but different seaside community. By day, we would sail, or go swimming; sometimes we would rent bikes, or just stroll around the quaint towns groping each other while window-shopping and eating ice cream. By night, we would make love on the boat surrounded by nothing but wind, sky and water. Sometimes we would have sex right out on the open deck under starry-lit skies and freshening summer breezes. But most times we would go below to the berth, where we would fill the mahogany cabin with noises of our lovemaking mixed with the sound of the boat rolling in the water.

Just when I thought it could not possibly get better it did. With each passing moment that we were together, we got closer and more comfortable together. And it was so much better than anything I could have imagined. When we made love, it was intense, each sexual encounter more mind-blowing than the last.

The two weeks with Matt were like a fairy-tale come true and he was my Prince and I was his Princess. It was with a heavy heart that we sailed back home to face reality, and a ticking clock that would send Matt back to college in just under three weeks.

Chapter 19: An Ass Kicking – June 2013

Current time. Sam confronts Brian for lying to Matt about them having sex.

A few days later, Matt tells Brian that he is dating Sam again and asks him for his thoughts. Matt lets Brian know he was confused after Sam's prom which led to his foul mood and the altercation.

Of course, Matt was confused at the time and assures Brian he never wants something like this to happen again. Matt confides to Brian – "Sam is the one for me".

Brian opens up to Matt and lets him know he was jealous of him and never wants someone to get in between them again. Matt opens up as well and lets him know how much he loves and respects him and wants him to find his forever gal.

Brian and Matt hug, it out. They both make a pact to one another that they will be there for each other no matter what happens going forward.

Chapter 20: The 'Cortship' ends – August 2005

Matt pulled the Range Rover to a complete stop in front of his parent's house and switched off the engine. We sat there for the longest time, not saying a word, just staring at each other and grinning like two fools in love.

"I'm going to grab my bags out of the trunk," he finally whispered.

"Okay," I whispered back, still smiling.

When he opened the passenger door for me, I suddenly got emotional, because I wasn't ready to face the outside world yet. Quite simply, it had been the best two weeks of my life. With a mixture of sadness and panic that gripped me, the fragile layer of insulation that we had wrapped ourselves in was now coming to an end.

He reached over, took one of my hands and slowly pulled it to his mouth, tenderly pressing the softest kiss there. The sweet gesture was so intimate, so perfect, that my tears began falling and I felt my heart racing in my chest.

He raised his hands and pressed them against my cheeks, wiping my tears with each of his thumbs. "Why are you crying?"

"Because I've never been happier," I said softly.

He kissed my hand again and then rumpled my hair affectionately. "The feeling is *very* mutual my crazy girl. But come on, we have a party to attend."

His parents were throwing us a party to celebrate our Beringer Bowl victory and all Cortship crew and their families had been invited to the festivities. Really, I think it was an excuse for Mrs. Cort to throw a big bash. She loved to entertain, and since Mr. Cort did not sail in the race himself this year, the party was a good opportunity for them to see some of the older sailors that they usually liked to socialize with during the summer race season.

The party was underway, and from the sound of things it was already in full swing, so I begrudgingly got out of the car, and headed up the path with Matt to the front door. Just before we entered the house, he raised his hand and tenderly caressed my cheek. Then his mouth was on mine. At first, his kiss was slow and measured, but then he deepened it, gently slamming my back into the door.

"Holy shit, Matt," I moaned into his mouth, my hands trembling as I placed them against his chest. "If you continue to kiss me like that, we'll never make it to the party."

"Sorry," he laughed as he buried his lips into my hair, before stepping back and loosening his grip. We stood there staring at each other, love-struck, with dreamy expressions on our faces and I felt myself blush.

"This summer was so great," he said, "being together. Being close to you, it was the best time of my life. I love you, Sam."

I was intoxicated by his words. "It was the best time of my life, too," I gushed, hugging him. We kissed. Then I started to grin from ear to ear. *He loves me.* All my insecurities went out the window, and I found my voice. "I love you, Matt. So much."

We walked into the party holding hands and I could feel my lips curving into a goofy grin. I was so ridiculously in love with this man, that it was insane. Soon, we were in the middle of the crowded living room, laughing with friends and acquaintances that kept congratulating us on winning the boat race. But before I knew it, we were separated. I lost track of him as I circulated through the party in a joyous haze moving from one group of friends to the next.

"Sammy!" Heather squealed, stepping forward and giving me a hug. "You're finally home. Where is Matt?"

"I don't know. I think maybe the kitchen," I said with a cheesy grin. "How are you?"

Heather took a step back and examined me closely. "Why the giddy grin? What's going on, Sam?"

Just returned from the race this past weekend.

"Nothing is going on, Heather. We just got home a few minutes ago."

"Sammy! Did you hook up with Matt?"

I didn't answer, but I was squirming from her scrutiny.

I heard Heather take a sharp intake of breath, and she looked concerned about something. "Listen Sammy, I need to warn you..."

But before she could speak, we were interrupted when a pair of large male hands wrapped around me from behind covering my eyes. Then a few seconds later, I heard the deep familiar voice of Brian yell, "Surprise!"

I giggled, "Oh - My God - Brian!!

I was caught off guard as his hands slid around my waist and he turned me around to face him, hugging me hard. "I've missed you, Slim!"

A feeling of guilt grew inside me, and I swallowed thickly, gently pulling away from Brian and taking a step back. "I thought you and Peter were not coming home for another week. This is such a surprise Brian, when did you guys get home?"

"We cut the trip early and arrived home two days ago so that we could be here for the party and surprise you. "I'm really proud of you, Slim, and so is Pete!"

"Where is Peter, anyway?" I asked, taking a deep breath as I tried to regain my thoughts. Matt and I had been so wrapped up in our own world that we hadn't really discussed how we were going to 'come out' and tell everyone that we were a couple. Guilt washed over me, because the last thing I wanted to do was to hurt Brian.

"Pete was hanging in the backyard with Laurel while she waited for Matt to get home."

"Laurel who?" I frowned. "Why is she waiting for Matt?"

"You know Laurel Adams from Stanford. Matt's…"

Heather abruptly stepped in between Brian and I. "Err…sorry to butt in Brian, but I need to talk to Sammy *now*," Heather said, grabbing my hand and dragging me away.

When we came to a complete stop by the staircase, Heather released me, but I noticed that she was frowning. "What's up, Heather?" I asked, tilting my head in confusion, waiting for her to respond.

"Sammy, I'm sure there is an innocent explanation, so don't flip out…" Heather began, hesitantly. "But there is something that you need to know…"

"Ok, you're starting to freak me out Heather. Why would I flip out?"

She laughed nervously. "I don't know how to say it Sam, so I'm just going to spit it out. Laurel Adams is Matt's friend from Stanford, and she flew in to surprise him. He wasn't expecting her…" Heather trailed off, looking sadly at me, something akin to pity in her eyes.

Suddenly my throat was bone-dry, and I was starting to have a bad feeling in the pit of my stomach. "When you say Matt's friend, what *exactly* do you mean?"

Heather cursed under her breath, and the look of sympathy on her face was so intense that it sent me reeling backwards and I stumbled. "Sammy are you okay?"

I closed my eyes as a sharp pang of jealousy shot through me. Then I slid past her in shock and denial, wanting to escape and find Matt. There had to be a reasonable explanation. Moving on autopilot, I made my way through the party with dulled senses, telling myself that everything would be ok, and almost believing it. When I reached the glass door that led to the backyard, I stared at the glass for a long time not wanting to face the awful mess that could be waiting for me on the other side.

Carefully, I opened the door and stepped onto the deck. It took a few minutes for my eyes to adjust to the sunlight, as I looked across the yard for Matt. As soon as I saw him, I saw Laurel Adams. She was a gorgeous blonde who had her arm possessively wrapped around Matt's waist and they were laughing, standing by the swimming pool, talking to my brother and his girlfriend, my parents, Mr. and Mrs. Cort, and another couple who I didn't recognize.

I stood there alone, feeling heartsick, but hopeful that there was an innocent explanation. I loved Matt and trusted him. I clung to the belief that he would never let me down, but even as I reassured myself, I was filled with suspicion and riddled with insecurity. My chest constricted and I felt like I could hardly breathe. "There you are," Brian said, coming to stand next to me on the deck. "Are you okay?"

"I don't know ... I think I might be getting sick."

"Do you want me to drive you home?" he asked, concerned. "You *do* look pale."

"Maybe, but I should say hello to Pete and my parents first," I said, heading toward the pool area, without waiting for his response.

"Will you wait up?" Brian yelled, catching up to me.

Up until that point, Matt had not seen us approach. But when he looked up and saw me, I immediately knew that something was wrong. His face was tense and reserved, and there was a flicker of remorse in his eyes. He looked like a guilty man!

Avoiding my eyes, Matt casually stepped away from the blonde's embrace. I let my eyes drop to my hands, as I took in a troubled breath.

"Look at you, winning on the open-water already!" Pete exclaimed, pulling me to him, and spinning me around. "Way to go, baby sister!"

"Don't spin her around Pete, she isn't feeling well." Brian said, protectively.

"What's wrong?" my mother asked, immediately concerned, placing her hand on my forehead to determine if I had a fever.

"I'm probably fine, just a scratchy throat and a headache," I lied. "Brian offered to drive me home so that I could get some rest."

"Are you sure you have to leave Samantha? Mrs. Cort asked. "Would you like to rest in the guest room? You might feel better after a nap."

"No thanks, I think I should go home."

"I'll take you," Matt stated. "It makes the most sense, because I already have your luggage and gear in my car."

I reacted quickly. "That would be great, Matt."

Brian shot Matt an irritated look, and he seemed pissed off. Then Brian turned to me. "Ok, Sam. I'll give you a call tomorrow."

The blonde looked upset and glared. "Matt, I've hardly seen you. I think you should let your brother drive her home."

Mrs. Cort was about to add her two cents, but before she had the opportunity to join the conversation, Matt cut her off. "It's a short drive, I'll be back soon."

Matt and I were about to take off when I summed up all my courage and I turned around and approached the blonde. "Hi, I'm Samantha Nottingham," I said in an unemotional voice, reaching out to shake her hand. "Who are you?"

"I'm Laurel Adams," she said defiantly, giving me a patronizing once-over, and tossing her long hair over her shoulder. "Matt's girlfriend from Stanford, and these are my parents," she pointed to the middle-age couple I didn't recognize, explaining that her dad and Mr. Cort were old college friends.

I wanted to slap the bitch or break down into heavy sobs. But instead, I somehow shook her hand and told them how nice it was to meet them. Then we said good-bye to everyone, and I followed Matt out to his car. Somehow, I managed to stay upright the entire time, with a slight smile on my face. Right then and there, I decided that I could have won an academy award for best actress for acting so normal when my world was crumbling beneath my feet.

We drove to my house in silence, gone was any hint of the love-struck bliss from our arrival only a short time ago. Neither of us said a word, as gut-wrenching tension filled the space between us.

Matt pulled up in front of my house and turned to me with sad eyes. "I'm sorry, Sam." His voice was barely audible.

My heart froze in my chest, but somehow, I found my voice. "Do you love her?"

"Of course not, Sam. I love you."

Reaching out, he took my hand, but I shrugged it away. "How long have you been together?" I asked, not trying to hide the hurt in my voice.

"A little over a year. I was going to tell you Sam, but…"

His answer stunned me, and I shook my head in disgust, trying to clear it. "But what Matt?" My tone was cold, filled with venom.

He was silent.

"Matt?"

"I don't know Sam. I wanted to tell you. I really did. I knew it was wrong, but things happened between us so fast, that I didn't know how to tell you. Then I decided I was going to break up with Laurel in September, so I thought…"

"You thought, what?" I asked, choking back tears.

"I was scared Sam. I know that sounds fucked up, but I didn't plan to fall in love with you. I was scared that if I told you the truth, I would lose you…"

It took a few minutes before I could speak and when I did, I acted tough as nails.

"So, you decided to lie and string me along instead?" I shouted, furious, feeling like a naive fool for trusting him. "It must have been a thrill for you to have your experienced college girlfriend waiting for you in California, while having a summer romance with me, your little innocent, schoolgirl friend."

The mood in the car was tense and I knew that I had wounded him with my vicious words, I could see it in his expression, and how he clenched his jaw. He was offended.

"It wasn't like that Sam. It wasn't premeditated. I did try to stay away from you at first, but then it just happened. I never meant to hurt anyone. Please believe me…"

"I can't believe anything you tell me anymore!" I yelled, letting out a shaky breath. "If Laurel hadn't shown up here, I never would have known that you were capable of such lies and manipulation. You're a *cheater*, and I don't trust you anymore!"

Quickly ending my tirade, I jerked the door open and stalked out of the car, slamming the door behind me. My feet were wobbly, and I was trembling as I hurried to the front door to escape him.

"Sam!" he shouted, but I ignored him as I fumbled for my house keys on the doorstep. "I have your bags. Will you please just give me a minute?"

I spun around to face him. "Was I just a booty call to you? A summer fling to keep you busy until you went back to Stanford?" I stepped forward and slapped him across the face. "Funny that you warned me to stay away from Tanner Harrington, at least with him, it was blindingly obvious what I was getting into. He never tried to *bullshit* me."

He stared at me shocked, touching his cheek where I had slapped him. "What? How could you think that?" he asked. His voice was strained, and he looked distraught. "I'm not perfect. I fucked up. But I told you the truth when I told you that I loved you. Please forgive me Sam?"

I shook my head numbly, staring blankly at him. "I can't Matt. Please go home."

He hesitated not moving from his spot, and that's when I begin to feel nauseous knowing that a breakdown was imminent. "Okay – I'll give you time to cool down," he murmured, smiling sadly and walking to his car.

Limply, I let myself in the house escaping to the safety of my bedroom before my family arrived home. I sank on my knees to the floor and screamed at the top of my lungs, filled with disappointment and despair over loving Matthew Cort for almost my entire life only to be confronted with the harsh reality of his betrayal. When I couldn't scream anymore, hot angry tears flowed uncontrollably down my cheeks, and I felt heartbroken and alone. For over a decade, I had placed Matt on a pedestal, and worshipped him like a hero, and it was a bitter pill to swallow to realize that the pedestal I placed him on was empty.

In that instant, my world changed, and I vowed never to let myself be a fool again.

Chapter 21: The Interview June 2013

Sam was excited about the opportunity that her dad introduced her to. He had a business associate who worked at an investment firm that specialized in socially responsible investing. Their market invests their clients' money in green companies, fair trade companies, and businesses that invest back into their communities.

Sam interviews and felt that she did well. Soon after, she is excited when she receives a phone call later that week letting her know they would like to invite her back for a second interview. They talk about her previous work with bitcoins and why she wants to work in this field of investing. Sam enjoys the conversation and likes the people. The following week, Sam receives an offer. She is stoked and can't wait to tell Matt.

When Matt phones later in the day, he sets up plans to meet in Central Park. After walking for a bit, Sam shares her news that she received a job offer and has accepted. Matt is happy. While he would have liked Sam to work with him, he knows she made the right choice.

Chapter 22: Heartsick – August 2005

I was curled up on the bedroom floor, trembling and crying, when I heard my bedroom door open. "Sam!" my mother choked out when she saw me. She took me in her arms and turned my face toward her. I struggled to pull myself up, gripping my mother's arm for balance and burying my tear-stricken face against her chest. "What's wrong?" she asked, her face drawn and etched with concern.

Like a tidal wave ready to burst, the dam broke, and I told my mother everything. Through choked sobs, I recounted the happy details of how I fell in love with Matt and the gut-wrenching pain I felt at finding out that he had a girlfriend the entire time we were together. I watched the different emotions displayed on my mother's face as she listened intently, and when I faltered, she urged me to continue with words of encouragement.

When I finished talking, I took in a succession of quick gasps of oxygen before a fresh round of tears assaulted me, rendering me frozen and incapable of further thought or communication. My mother cooed words of love and support in my ear and helped me into bed. There I succumbed into a fitful night of sleep. For a short stint, my dreams provided relief. I dreamed of Matt holding me. His hands. His voice. His smell. It all seemed so real, but then I woke up, and an overwhelming sense of anger and grief hit me again, knocking me down, and leaving me hopeless.

The next morning, which was Sunday, I sat in my old ratty pajamas in the kitchen staring at the wall and wiping at the tears on my face with the palm of my hand. I watched while my uneaten cheerios got soggy as I repeatedly pushed them in and out of the milk with my spoon. I had no desire to eat. In fact, I had no desire to do anything, except feel sorry for myself.

Every few minutes my mother would come in and hover over me. But she let me wallow in my misery for hours on end, without disturbing me. Sometime later, I heard her whispering in hushed tones to my dad and brother. Peter hissed out a stream of profanities. "I'm going to kill the SOB!" he screamed, and I heard the front door slam behind him. Then the house was silent again, despite the occasional intrusion of my mom and dad checking in on me.

About an hour later, Peter stormed into the house, setting off a chain reaction of phone calls and impromptu visits from every member of the Cort family. But I had no interest in speaking to anyone, especially Matt, so I closed myself off, and avoided everyone like the plague.

Monday was a carbon copy of the previous day. The only significant difference was that I received a huge bouquet of flowers from Matt with a card.

Sam,

Please forgive me.

I love you.

Matt

I ripped up his note and threw the flowers away.

By Wednesday morning, the initial shock had worn off, and my tears had dried up, but I did not feel any better. I took a shower and got dressed in an effort to stop dwelling on my misery and appear somewhat normal in front of my family. I had started to eat again, gorging myself on comfort food like ice cream and cookies, but I felt totally exhausted, after yet, another sleepless night of tossing and turning. My anxiety was crippling and on the rise. I was plagued by constant worry and bleak thoughts over my feelings for Matt. *Literally, I felt damned if I do, damned if I don't.* There was no comfortable solution to the dilemma I now faced. I could not imagine my life without him; just the thought of it made me panic-stricken. I had never felt as alive, and happy, as I did with Matt. But for the first time in my life, I questioned whether he was *actually* good for me. The pull towards him had always been so intense and automatic. But now I was plagued with doubts. I felt bamboozled and taken in, and I could not escape the grim reality that I no longer trusted him, nor at that moment, liked him.

By Wednesday afternoon, I grew restless and finally built up the courage to check my cell phone for messages. My voice mailbox was full, and I had received a ton of text and email messages. With a heavy heart, I started to scroll through them, starting first with voicemail. The first message was from Heather late Saturday afternoon…

"Hey, Sam. It's me. I heard you left the party not feeling well. I'm worried about you. Please call me back."

I sighed and deleted her message, going on to the next message, which was from Brian later Saturday evening…

"Hi, Slim! Wanted to see how you were feeling? Also, are you free Wednesday night? Because I'm planning to dazzle you once you say yes to our first date! Anyway, give me a call tomorrow, and hopefully we can hang out?"

I deleted Brian's message feeling an intense amount of guilt, and biting my lip, wondering how I was ever going to face him. Going on to listen to my third message, it was from Heather again, this time, late Saturday night….

"Holy shit, girl! Matt stumbled home drunk like five hours after dropping you off. When he finally got home, all hell broke loose and he very ungentlemanly broke up with a very pissed off Laurel Adams. It was really awkward for my parents, and Mr. and Mrs. Adams, because they were planning to stay here in our guest room, but after the fight, they quickly left with their daughter to a hotel. Wow... was it ugly. Call me and I'll give you all the juicy details!"

The next message was from Matt on Sunday morning and he sounded like shit. His voice was raspy, with a sad and tormented edge to it. Good. I hope he was suffering for all the pain he inflicted. (The untrustworthy bastard!)

"Sam, it's me. I know that you don't want to talk to me right now and that I hurt you, and I'm sorry. I know I fucked up, but I'm begging you to give me a chance to explain. Please? (Long pause and then he lowered his voice). I broke everything off with Laurel last night. I know it seems way too little, way too late, and I'm sorry about that. If I could go back to the beginning, I would do things differently. I know I don't deserve

your forgiveness, but please let me apologize face to face. I love you, Sam. Please give me a chance to fix this. Please."

The fifth message was from Heather, later Sunday afternoon....

"Sam, what the hell is going on? Will you please call me as soon as you get this message! Peter was here and he was pissed, screaming his head off. Long story short, Peter went ape shit on Matt and punched him, and Matt just took it, not defending himself, until my dad pulled Peter off him. Ah...I...um...I'm guessing you really did hook up with Matt this summer and that this has to do with the Laurel Adams thing? Hey...I'm not defending what Matt did, but he is really depressed so could you throw hiim a bone and at least talk to him? Also, I think you should call Brian, because um...he is really upset about this whole thing. In fact, Brian also tried to beat the crap out of Matt, but my dad broke that fight up too. It's like a bad nightmare around here, Sam. Just give me a call when you can.

The sixth message was from Brian, Monday afternoon. His tone was reserved, bordering on cold...

"Hey Slim, It's me Brian. I heard what happened. (Clears his throat) I think we should talk. Give me a call."

The seventh message was from Matt, late Tuesday night. His voice was low, and he sounded nervous…

"Hey Sam…It's me…Matt. I know I'm the last person on Earth that you want to talk to right now. (Laughing nervously). I've been trying to give you space, but I really think we should talk. (Long pause) I can't eat, I can't sleep. I miss you, baby, and I'm so sorry that I hurt you. Please call me, yell at me, hit me, or do something…anything, but just stop ignoring me. If I don't hear from you by tomorrow, I'm going to come by your house so that we can talk."

With a shaky hand, I anxiously clutched my phone to my chest, and I could feel the butterflies in my stomach as I texted Matt.

I received your messages, but I can't see you right now. Please respect my wishes and DO NOT come over.

Matt quickly replied.

I will respect your wishes Sam, but you can't avoid me forever. We NEED to talk.

***

I picked up the phone, and with trembling fingers, I dialed Heather's number and asked her if she wanted to come over. When Heather arrived at my house, she wrapped me in a hug, and tenderly squeezed me. She clutched my hand and we walked to the backyard, sitting together on the stone wall that encircled the patio and fire pit. The sun was at our backs and it felt good to be outside in the late afternoon warmth. We let our shoes fall to the hot ground and dangled our bare feet in silence. I closed my eyes and leaned back enjoying the sun on my face. "How are you?" Heather asked.

"I don't know," I stated flatly. The weeds growing in the gaps in the wall preoccupied me and I started pulling at them in hopes of channeling some of my frustration. "Fuck." I finally swore under my breath. "Do your parents and Brian know everything that happened between Matt and me?"

"Pretty much," she confirmed. "I'm sorry that Matt was such an asshole. We are all pissed at him. If it makes you feel better, you've missed a couple of priceless moments!"

"How priceless?"

"Well, let's just say he's gotten his ass chewed out a lot!"

I raised an eyebrow an amusement, and for the first time in days, I felt myself smile, lifting my mood fractionally. But the relief was temporary, so I distracted myself with pulling weeds again, which helped take the edge off my anger and irritability.

"I'm seriously, worried about you Sam," she said. "Do you want to talk about it?"

"I'm not sure what to say," I admitted, shrugging my shoulders. "It's complicated."

"Ha! That's an understatement and we haven't even talked about Brian yet." She frowned at me. "Listen Sam, I know that you've liked Matt forever, and the chemistry between you two this summer could melt an iceberg in seconds. But, you know, just as well as I do, how many girls Matt has been with.

He's not perfect, and you need to open your eyes and stop hero-worshipping him. That being said, I think you guys could be the real deal; so you should talk to him and give him a chance to make up for his mistake."

"It's not that simple." I scowled.

"Do you love him?" She asked bluntly.

I shifted uncomfortably, letting out a soft sigh as I remembered various tender moments with Matt over the years. "Of course, I love him." I told her quietly. "But what difference does that make? Matt has been lying to me this whole time, and I feel like a naïve fool for trusting him. I thought that what we had was special, but I feel duped, even worse, I feel like a slut for being put in the position of being the *other woman*. He doesn't deserve my love, and things are probably fucked up beyond repair with us."

"Are you sure? Don't give up."

I said nothing and there was silence for a few minutes. The problem was that I no longer trusted Matt and I wasn't sure that I would ever be able to relax around him again. My defenses were up, and I could feel myself closing down. There was nothing left to say.

"What about Brian?" Heather said at last. "Have you spoken to him yet."

"No," I replied automatically. "But I will."

"When?"

"There's no time like the present," I joked weakly, feeling the guilt began to coil in my stomach over the thought of facing him. I knew that I couldn't avoid him forever, but I was dreading *it*. I told myself that somehow, I would make it up to Brian. But of all the boys in the world that I could have fallen in love with, over him, I chose his brother, his one Achilles heel. How could I make up for that?

***

The next morning, I was scheduled to meet Brian at Crocker Park. The park was one of my favorite spots in town, because it offered sweeping views of the entire harbor and had lots of benches, grassy areas, and rocks to chill and hang out on. When I got there, Brian hadn't arrived yet, so I took the rocky staircase down to the water's edge, and sat on the pavement, dangling my feet above the calm waters of the Atlantic Ocean. My stomach was twisted in knots and I was filled with trepidation, but I took a few deep breaths and forced myself to calm down as I contemplated what I would say to him. I heard footsteps behind me, and immediately knew it was him. I turned and froze when I saw his hard expression. He looked incredibly hurt and angry. I scooted over to make room for him next to me on the hot, rough pavement. "Hey there, Brian."

"Hey," he answered, taking a seat, his eyes wide and wounded. "You should have told me about you and Matt. It wasn't cool how I found out."

"I know and I'm sorry. I was planning to tell you, I just...I just didn't know how." I lowered my eyes to the ground, feeling an acute stab of guilt and shame hit me hard. "Please don't hate me Brian," I groveled.

"I could never hate you, Sam, but I feel stupid that I've chased you for months, when all along you've had the hots for my brother. The worst part was that I never even saw it coming!"

I made a derisive snort. "Well, that makes two of us!"

Brian shrugged. "Come on, Slim, you can't be surprised that he was cheating. Matt always wants more and he's always pushing boundaries. You know as well as I do that he moves from girl to girl and never sticks around very long."

"But I thought..." I took a moment to clear my painful thoughts, "that what we had was different."

"I'm sure he cares for you, Sam, but Matt is complicated." Brian's chest was rising and falling rapidly. "Are you going to forgive him?" He asked bluntly, his question brimming with hostility.

I felt my brow furrow and my tears began falling. "I don't think I can." I answered shakily, my voice thick with emotion.

"Good," he said, unable to disguise his obvious relief.

When the last of my tears had dried, Brian made a peace offering and stretched out his hand to me. "Let's go for a walk."

I nodded, accepting his peace offering and his hand.

Chapter 23: Senior Year – October 2005

I was in a funk. Or maybe it was considered a rut? Whatever one called it; it didn't feel good. The very fact that I still felt so melancholy about Matt lying to me was dragging me down. It was like I lost a part of me that day, and all my dreams went poof, vanishing before my eyes.

Since childhood, I had wanted Matt. Always. Matt had filled every desire, every wish, and every dream I had about love and the future. I had wanted him to love me, and he did. But the end result was not what I expected. Now I found myself questioning everything, wondering how I could have been so wrong about him. I felt unbelievably morose.

I should have been happy that it was my senior year of high school, but instead I felt numb and confused. Adding to my mood was the fact that I felt alone. Peter, Brian, and Matt were away at college and I was avoiding Heather like the plague. I knew none of this was her fault, but sometimes being around her, made me feel even sadder. She reminded me of her brother, and I just needed some space.

The breakup had been excruciating.

"She doesn't want to see you!" I heard Peter say to Matt for the twelfth consecutive night in a row. Matt had shown up on our doorstep every night for two weeks and I felt bad for the obvious strain I was putting on my family. Everyone was feeling awkward right now and the tension was thick. I knew he was leaving for Stanford in a couple of days and that I had to face him, but the situation was awful, and I was unsure of myself.

Regardless, I knew that it was time to confront him. I froze for one terrified moment, before leaving the safety of my bedroom. "It's alright, Pete. I'll talk to him," I said as I approached the front entrance of the house and stepped onto the porch.

"Are you sure?" Peter asked.

I glanced at my brother and gave him a little smile. "I'm sure."

Peter jerked his head in Matt's direction. "Don't fuck with my sister, Matt. You hear me?"

I glanced at Matt and he looked even more miserable than I felt. "I have no intention of hurting your sister."

A tense moment passed, and Peter finally turned to go. "I'm leaving."

Matt and I watched in silence as Peter retreated, and then we both stood on the front porch staring at each other. It was incredibly uncomfortable. Finally, I recovered and broke eye contact. I closed the door to give us some privacy and took a seat on the front steps. It seemed like it took forever before Matt followed me and cautiously sat down next to me.

I warily eyed him and was surprised by what I saw. The wildly charismatic and confident Matt had vanished. He seemed nervous - "Sam?"

"Hey, Matt. Um," I stumbled over my words, trying to ease the weird tension that now existed between us. "That's quite a bruise you have there. Does it hurt?"

"Which one?"

"Oh, well, um…" For the first time, I noticed just how banged up his face really was. He had a purple bruise on the side of his jaw and another one below his right eye. "You look like hell. Was it Pete or Brian who caused this?"

"Wh-what?" he asked. "You heard about that?"

"Yeah, I heard the story. Why didn't you defend yourself and fight back?"

He absently rubbed his fingers on his bruised skin. "It looks worse than it feels."

"You didn't answer my question?"

He shrugged. "Don't worry about the bruises, Sam. I deserved that," he said with disgust. Then he turned his head to me, reaching up and grabbing my hand. "If you heard about the fights, then you must know that I broke up with Laurel.

"Really, Matt? You've come here every night and incessantly called and emailed me. Is that the best you can come up with?"

"No," he said quietly through clenched teeth. "I'm sorry, Sam. Please let me explain. It's not what you think."

"Bullshit! You've had all fucking summer to tell me the truth, Matt. Stop lying to me!"

"Sam, it's not like that. I never planned for any of this to happen. The last thing I wanted was to hurt you," he rambled. "I know I fucked up, but I love you, Sam. Please let me explain everything."

"No." I cried. "I don't want to hear it." I choked, struggling to keep my anger at bay.

Matt put his arm around my shoulder trying to comfort me and said, "Look, Sam. I don't want to make you upset, but I love you and that's the truth. I'm sorry that I wasn't straight with you from the beginning but let me make things right. I know I can do better. Please don't end this."

I shook my head, while tears streamed down my face. "I can't be with someone I don't trust."

"So, I'm guilty and that's the verdict?" Matt laughed, a sad, defeated laugh, and shook his head. "You're just going to throw the key away with no possibility of parole then?"

I shrugged at him, pulling away from his embrace. "You're the asshole, Matt, so don't try to act so pure and innocent."

Matt caught my arm with a shivering hand. "Can we please just talk about this?"

I closed my eyes, knowing I'd come to the moment of truth. *Could I forgive him?* I wanted more time to think. I was still unquestionably drawn to him, but for the first time in my life, I doubted his sincerity. As much as I would have loved to forgive and forget and start over with him, I just didn't know if he was good for me. And anyway, he was going to college some 3,000 miles away. Sure, he would come home every now and then, but what kind of relationship could we have long distance. Besides, he would graduate in June and I would have to leave for college next year. Obviously, the odds were against us – we just weren't right for each other. I cleared my throat, licked my lips, and stalled for a few final seconds. "I'm sorry," I said weakly and wiped the tears pooling in my eyes.

"Sam, please don't do this!" he said, his voice growing progressively louder, more distressed. "You're making a mistake."

Overcome with heartbreak, but trying desperately to cling to my resolve, I ignored him and stood up.

"Sam!" He yelled, but I didn't answer and walked stoically toward the door.

Before I went inside, I turned and looked at him one last time. "You really hurt me, Matt." I choked out. "I hope someday that we can be friends again, but right now, I'm so fucking angry with you. Please don't contact me again."

***

Chapter 24: Reflections – August 2013

Sam was really enjoying her work. And, she took pride in her professional life and was well-respected by her colleagues. She was confident, successful, and was living a great life.

Heather was still her best friend. From that day many years ago when she climbed the tree in the Cort's backyard and fell into Matt's hand, she knew he was special. Life with Matt, Brian, and their BBB sister, blonde, beautiful, and bold Heather was her life. They were forever intertwined.

However, she wanted more, to get married, have children, and a house with the white picket fence.

Success was great but Sam knew that her job did not define who she was. It gave her the means to be the woman she wanted to be.

She was in love with Matt. She enjoyed every moment she was with him. She loved the way he laughed, the way he held her when they danced, and she loved watching him as he slept.

She didn't date anyone else since they reconnected in London. However, she couldn't wait for him forever.

It was a beautiful Saturday night. Sam and Matt were enjoying the street life of New York.

"Where are we going?" asked Sam.

"Let's get something to eat."

Sam had a feeling that something was up.

Sam knew her relationship with Matt was strong. Working at separate companies gave Sam the confidence and the opportunity to make a name for herself. It also strengthened her relationship with Matt. She saw Matt socially and didn't have to worry about managing both a work and romantic relationship with him.

"So, where are we going to eat?"

"I found a nice place in Greenwich Village. It's called Label's."

"Never heard of it."

"You'll like it."

Sam knew something was up.

Label's was a small, nice restaurant that had impromptu jazz sessions and comedians. Good food. It was a place that was easy to walk by, but once you found it, it was a place you remembered. Label's didn't have scheduled performances, musicians or comedians. They just came in, set up, and performed.

Sam loved the place. She also knew Matt was up to something.

The entertainment began with a jazz duo, and Israeli bassist and a Japanese pianist.

"They are going to be famous", said Matt.

"How do you know?"

"Watch as they play. They have a great sense of communication. Either one can finish the thought of the other. You can see it as they look at each other."

Sam watched and saw what Matt meant. It was the same as their relationship. They could just look at each other and know what the other person thought.

She looked at Matt and knew he was going to ask her to marry him.

The jazz duo played two sets. A comedian came on next. He joked about love, romance, and marriage.

Sam looked at Matt.

"What?" asked Matt.

"Oh, nothing."

Some nice music, sense of communication, jokes about love, romance, and marriage. Did Matt know the performers? Had Matt planned this?

They walked to Washington Square Park. Matt got down on one knee.

"We've known each other for a long time, the way we think, what makes us laugh and cry. Sam, you bring joy in my life. You have from the day I first met you. You make me laugh. You make me smile. Will you give me the honor of being your husband? Will you marry me?"

"Yes."

A few weeks later, Sam and Matt have a dinner party and Brian toasts the couple and they all want to be involved in their newfound joy. Sam and Matt move ahead and plan a gorgeous wedding and worldwide honeymoon.

Five years later – the two are happily married and after welcoming their first son, Nick, Sam learns that she is expecting again. Six months later, they welcome their second son, Jack. The following Summer, the families have a reunion at their Summer house in Montauk Coast and their vessel is named Nick and Jack.

CPSIA information can be obtained
at www.ICGtesting.com
Printed in the USA
BVHW031151251019
562081BV00001B/4/P